ONE LIFE TO GET RIGHT

A CRIME NOVEL

BY COREY GARMON

PROLOGUE

"Mr. Hawkins," Judge Bates said. "I really don't have any clue as to why I'm giving you this judicial release. Your record is definitely one of a kind. You seem to feel as if selling drugs is the only career for you in this life, and as many times as you've been caught, I don't see why.

"However, your lawyer, whom you should thank after this proceeding is finished, has shown me that you do have some kind of sense after all. The court is pleased to hear that you own your own business. More importantly, you realize what you're doing is causing yourself destruction," the judge reassured. "Let me assure you Mr. Hawkins, I will give you every minute of incarceration that you have coming to you provided you step into this courtroom again."

Judge Bates looked over the rim of his outdated plastic frames — paused for an effect — then continued: "You shouldn't so much as come to a friends' sentencing in the future for it may affect how I sentence him," said the judge. "Do you understand?"

"Yes sir," Mr. Hawkins said.

"Good," Judge Bates said. "Now as you know, if you violate any terms of this release I can give you up to one year in prison for the offense you are here for today. In addition to that year, I can give you from one, up to three years for violating this release. This will not include the time you'll receive for the new crime that you may have committed. Is that clear?"

"Yes sir." Hawkins humbly replied.

He zoned out — rambling a yes sir at every pause. He was so happy to be coming home. He'd only been locked up for four months. Out of all the time he'd done in the prison system, those four months were the worse. Nothing happened. No fights. No deaths in the family — though close. No extortion attempts. Nothing.

Before Malik Hawkins caught his case, his life was running smooth. He'd bought his own business. He was stacking money. Just had his first child. Things were on the up, yet he was powerless at sentencing.

"Mr. Hawkins," the judge said. "You're free to go."

After waiting for paper work, and seeing his parole officer, Malik desperately wanted to see his daughter. Her mom brought her to his home. Malik fell in love all over again.

He adored Dejanique and from that day forward he vowed to never leave her again. Malik ran his hands through the head full of hair Dejanique already had. He was in awe of the honey complexion and big brown eyes as if he'd never seen her before. She was perfect.

Now that his freedom was restored, he realized who was really in control. Not Judge Bates. Not his parole officer. Not his lawyer or his daughter's mom:

"Our Father, who art in heaven, hallowed be thy name. Thy kingdom come. Thy will be done, on earth as it is in heaven.

Give us this day our daily bread. And forgive us our trespasses, as we forgive those who trespass against us. And lead us not into temptation, but deliver us from evil. For thine is the kingdom, and the power, and the glory, forever. AMEN!"

THREE MONTHS LATER

The barbershop was slow on a Tuesday afternoon. The day was wet and gray. Clouds loomed over Toledo, Ohio as if they were there to stay. Malik looked himself over in the mirror, decided he needed to shave his face, and line his mustache. His reflection shot back a dark, bald headed brother, wide African nose, big brown eyes, and facial hairs growing out of an otherwise smooth face. He went to work using his Andis liners, snatched a neck strip out of its holder, doused it with liquid razor and lined himself with perfection.

"Um hmm," Malik hummed with approval at a job well done.

Jerry walked in.

"Wutupdoe," Jerry said. "Damn, where everybody at?"

"Niggas got hungry I guess," Malik said. "Chuck and 'L' went to lunch. I just got here fa real. Thought I was missin sumthin ... guess not."

Jerry laughed, taking off his coat. Jerry was also a chocolate brother, somewhat lighter than Malik. He was about six foot three, waves in his hair, small brown beady eyes, small nose, and a big-thick neck like a boxer. He wore a black jogging suit and a pair of white and black Jordan IV's.

"Sheeeiit, we know you aint missin' shit. Rain, sleet, or snow, you gon' be getting it mufucka," said Jerry. "Aye doe, get me together real quick?"

"What you tryna do?" Malik asked.

"Low taper, on the back and the sides—crispy lining."

"It's on," Malik said.

Malik brushed off his clippers and liners, sprayed disinfectant on them, snapped on a two guard and went to work.

"Aye Malik," asked Jerry.

"Wut up?" Malik countered.

"Why you always gotta be so fly in this mufucka?" Jerry chuckled. "I mean you got ya lil' white thermal on—First of all, who cut hair in white anyway?

"Then you got ya blue Yankee fitted on, blue Pelle jeans, wheat and white Timbos? I'm sayin doe, why can't you just be regular nigga?"

"Damn, I mean," Malik said laughingly. "I aint know you was checkin for me like that, pink team ass nigga. I am regular.

"You act like I got my jewels on, and my stunner shades," he continued. "Shit, jeans, boots, thermal, it's cold, raining—what the fuck I'm sposed' to have on?"

"You know what I mean," Jerry said. "You … ."

The conversation was interrupted. Both men looked towards the door, and for good reason. In walked a set of the curviest hips either man had seen in a long while. Her straight hair lay perfectly across her caramel face. Malik could tell she wore a taper in the back. Her thick full lips looked saturated with lip-gloss and her eyes were a very light brown, almost hazel but not quite. She wore a simple pair of Seven jeans, a thin cream sweater, brown leather jacket, and matching boots.

"Are you guys taking walk-ins or do I need to make an appointment," she said.

"Naw, we open," answered Malik. "Who are you looking for?"

"Nobody really," she said. "I just left Amigos, and saw it was a shop down here … decided to get my taper cleaned up. Can you get me in?"

"I don't see why not," Malik said. "Let me get him out the way and I'll be right with you."

"Oh I'm not in any rush," said the mystery woman. "Take your time."

"Yea, she'll wait Malik," Jerry chimed in with a devilish look.

Malik tapered Jerry with intense concentration, and lined him up with the precision of a surgeon. Malik passed Jerry the mirror.

"You cool?" he asked.

"Oh fa sho," laughed Jerry, as he passed Malik a twenty. "Damn I might have to go to two dollar Tuesday or sumthin now. Good lookin. Holla at me tomorrow bout that fam."

Malik turned around to conceal the smirk on his face, knowing Jerry was on some bullshit.

"I'm ready," Malik said to the woman.

"How are you? I'm Melissa," she spoke.

Melissa stretched out her hand, offering a shake. Malik couldn't help but to notice her manicured fingernails. As he shook Melissa's hand, he noticed of her soft skin. The scent of the creed that floated from her body. He was instantly aroused.

"Nice to meet you, I'm Malik," he replied.

Malik knew he'd be done in a matter of minutes. He tried to find an angle. They talked about her being a student and interning as a paralegal, which interested Malik a lot, but he wasn't ready for that conversation, yet. They talked about Barack Obama. Great conversation, but that wasn't it. Finally, they spoke about Toledo's nightlife … or the lack thereof.

"Where you be hanging out at?" asked Malik.

"Nowhere really," she said. "If I do go somewhere it would probably be the Classic, or Our Brothers Place on Huron. What you know about that?"

Malik laughed.

"Nothing really," Malik said. "Except it's my uncle's spot."

"Seriously?" asked Melissa.

"Yup," boasted Malik. "I've never seen you at none of those spots though. And I'm positive I would've remembered you."

She smiled.

"I aint say I be there every week, just when I need a break from all that damn studying."

"What you going to school for?" asked Malik.

"Criminal Justice," Melissa said. "That shits too stressful. I don't have much time to do anything."

"Hence, the paralegal internship—let me be the first to congratulate you on your future success," said Malik.

"Thank you," Melissa replied.

"So, what you got going on tonight?" asked Malik.

Melissa smiled again, this time uncontrollably. She exposed her deep dimples and smile that shined brighter than gold.

"Not much of anything. I'll probably end up at home watching television. I swear. You probably think I'm lying, but I'm really a prude," she said.

"You like sports?" Malik asked.

"What kind?"

"Basketball."

"Yup, sure do. Especially Allen Iverson," said Melissa smiling from ear to ear.

Malik laughed as he watched Melissa mimic a jump shot.

"Oh yea, I didn't think he was a sport," Malik said mockingly.

"You know what I mean," she laughed.

"Well listen I got these tickets to see the Cavs tonight," said Malik. "I know we just met, but I'm diggin' you right now. I don't bite. I swear I don't, it's just one date.

"Okay," said Melissa.

"You can bring someone else if you'd li--," at that moment, Malik realized she'd agreed. "Okay then, that's what's up."

"What time the game start?" asked Melissa.

"Like, eight."

"You got a card or something?" she asked.

He gave her his card.

"I'll call you when I'm ready," she said.

"Please do. I'm leaving early anyway," said Malik.

Melissa gave Malik a look that he thought indicated her attraction towards him. Malik didn't know the look was because she wondered if he always came to work so well dressed. Melissa tucked the card in her purse and walked away.

"See you later," Melissa said smiling.

"Damn," mumbled Malik, as her backside kept him mesmerized.

*

Chuck and L walked in just as Melissa hopped in her white 2008 Chevy Monte Carlo. Chuck was a big dark skinned brother, about six feet tall and over two hundred pounds. He kept his braids clean and in a design.

L was slightly shorter than Chuck — skinny as Snoop Dogg, light brown, with 360 waves. Even though L was skinny, he had an appetite that couldn't be matched. He was always hungry. He took off his gray sweatshirt, matching his gray Pelle jogging suit, and black and gray Nike Air Max 95'.

"Who the fuck was that Malik?" asked L, stuffing his boneless chicken in his mouth.

"Ha," Malik blurted out. "Don't you worry about that playa, I think I might wife her."

"Damn," said Chuck. "Like that? She was cold. Who is she though? Old flame? What? Holla atcha fam."

"Naw I just met her for real," explained Malik. "She came in trying to get a taper, comin' from Amigo's and shit. I was getting Jerry together when she walked in looking like something outta Essence. Me and Jerry was star struck like a mufucka."

The rest of the day was uneventful. Malik cut a couple more heads. Literally, two, and decided he would leave early like he planned. Chuck and L were still cutting hair when he got finished. Malik cleaned up, and grabbed his coat.

"You out?" asked Chuck.

"Yes sir," said Malik. "Hold it down."

"You tryna get on this game later?" asked L.

"I gotta shoot a couple of moves and then I'm supposed to get up with ole girl, so shit, if it ... ."

"Aw shit I forgot that fast," said L. "It's on."

Malik walked outside and hopped into his black 08' Ford F-150. He turned up the T.I. c.d. that was already in the deck. Rhianna sang:

Jus live ya life….. Aye

As Malik pulled off his phone rang.

"Hello," said Malik. He paused, "who dis?"

He listened.

"The same way—that's what's up. Gimme twenty minutes," said Malik.

Rhianna continued:

We'll be posted up on the top spot livin my life, my life

*

Boom! Boom! Boom!

Tony's Desert Eagle rang out loud — his bullets only missing their target by millimeters.

"Bitch ass nigga, "Tony continued dumping. Boom! Boom! "Don't ever pull no strap on me and not use it bitch."

Tony ran after the young man that hit him in the back of the head two weeks before. Tony was furious. His head bled through his braids, but his rage didn't subside once the pain ended.

In between then and now Rod called Tony bragging and telling him he'd murk Tony if he tried to come after him. But Tony was a vet, Rod was a rookie, trying to earn some stripes. This is why he almost shit on himself when Tony crept up on him on foot.

Boom! Boom!

The .50 caliber interrupted the noise of the daily Hill Avenue traffic. Rod ran into the apartments next to the corner store. He knocked on a crackhead's door. The crackhead let him in just before Tony came around the corner.

Tony looked to the right, then left. He looked under cars, and between bushes. Satisfied Rod wouldn't be sneaking up on him, he left. Tony came to the realization this was Rod's stomping ground.

"I'll catch him," Tony said to himself.

He tucked his ferocious weapon in his waistband, pulled his shirt over the bulge, zipped up his jacket, and headed to his car.

Tony sped off in his rental car, a black Cadillac DTS. He called his homeboy from that area.

"What's good boy," Malik answered.

'What's good bro," asked Tony. "You at work?"

"Naw, just left about ten, fifteen minutes ago. Bout to shoot this lil' demo real quick," said Malik. "Da fuck you do now?"

Tony smiled on the other end of the phone.

"Da fuck make you think you know me," said Tony laughing.

"I can hear it in your voice," Malik said.

"I bet," said Tony. "Man why I almost crack ya boy head."

Malik remembered the night, a couple of weeks before when Tony came over his house at four in the morning, head leaking — strangely calm telling everything that happened.

"You caught his lil' young ass," asked Malik.

"You know I don't play no games," Tony replied.

Tony's train of thought was interrupted by the Toledo Police Department behind him. Their lights flashed, signaling him to pull over. He thought for a brief second ... pistol on his waist, on parole ... he smashed the gas.

"Bro I'm getting sweated by the hook right now. I'm bout to pop out over by yo people crib. Come get me."

"Stay on the phone so I know where you at," said Malik.

Tony turned down Carol Lane. The DTS held well in the rain. He sped down the street making a sharp left turn. The

Caddy fishtailed slightly, but the police were at least four car lengths behind. Their Dodge Charger didn't handle as well as the Cadillac. Tony slowed around a series of curves and left handed turns. The police kept up for the most part until the slickness of the road caused them to slide into a light pole. Tony turned around a couple more corners and jumped out of the car. Fleeing on foot, he threw the pistol on the ground, kicking it into a sewer near him.

"Hello?" Tony asked, never breaking stride.

He breathed through his nose like a well-conditioned athlete.

"Yeah," Malik answered. "It's 6-4-5-5."

"6-4-5-5?" repeated Tony.

"Yeah, I'll be there in like two minutes," said Malik.

Tony made it to his destination found the keypad and punched as fast as he could. The garage wasn't all the way open, before Tony slid underneath the door. Tony found the keypad on the inside of the garage and immediately closed the door.

"Whew," Tony sighed in relief.

Malik pulled up right behind him. He saw the police, now four or five cars deep, eyeing him as if he was the suspect.

"I saw him run through here," said one officer, pointing towards Malik. "Sir, excuse me sir."

"Yes," said Malik.

"Hi, I'm officer Brown," as he extended his hand.

Malik grabbed his laptop bag and cell phone.

"Sorry my hands are full. Can I help you?" he asked.

Officer Brown took note of the gesture, but thought nothing of it. No one likes the police nowadays.

"Yeah, I was chasing a suspect from a shooting earlier on and I kinda think he may be in your backyard or in your garage."

"Oh," Malik pretended to be surprised. "Well you can check the backyard, but I never leave this garage open. As a matter of fact—look," he pointed to the keypad. "The only way to get in is with a garage door opener, or if you use the keypad. Only my mom and I have the code. If someone did get in here the alarm would've sounded."

Malik shrugged his shoulders.

"Sorry. Hope you catch the dummy."

"I see," Officer Brown responded. "Well considering we haven't gotten that call, I guess you're right. Sorry to bother you."

"Sorry I couldn't have been more help," Malik said.

"Its okay," said the officer warming up to Malik. "Thanks anyway, if you see anything give us a call."

"Will do officer."

Malik used his key to get in the house. To his surprise, Tony already had his shoes off in the basement watching television.

"Da fuck you doin dude," Malik laughed.

"Shit I got my shoes off," Tony said. "You know Ms. Diane don't play that shit."

"Don't be leavin' me out there to clean up yo bullshit, nicca."

Malik opened his laptop case and pulled out its contents: one laptop, and nine ounces of cocaine.

"Damn," said Tony. "You a cool, smooth muthafucka. I saw you pull that shit out the truck. You aint even blink. Where you get that from doe?"

"Oh, I been had this from my last play," Malik said. "I was about to dump this shit on my man before you called chump. Got me ridin around crazy than a muthafucka, and you better hope these niggas get tired soon before I turn your ass in. I got a hot date at eight can't be late! Great! Great! Great!"

They laughed at Malik's' latest rendition of Eddie Murphy.

"Whatever dude," said Tony. "You always tryna fuck on sumthin, lil' sneaky mufucka."

"Don't try to get off the subject," Malik re-iterated. "Nigga, what happened?"

Tony twisted his lips, blew out a deep breath, and tilted his head as if that's how he re-wound his thoughts.

"Man I was out this way right, tryna see what's up wit my nigga wit that purp. I wasn't thinkin about this nigga. Came to check out a picture this nigga had foe me, get a number and stab out," Tony said. "After I do that I couldn't believe I saw this nigga tryna politic on some ass at the Hill Store."

Tony went on to explain the situation as animated as he could.

Tony was a pretty boy. High yellow, long braids, he kept well-groomed, stocky build and about 5 feet 9 inches He took care of himself, so he couldn't stand for a nigga trying to get at him. He wasn't going for it. It was a blow to his ego. One he wouldn't take lightly.

The police finally left after an hour. Tony watched his rental car get towed on a flatbed back to the police impound. Malik dumped his package as soon as they left, and dropped off Tony soon after that.

Melissa called Malik to see if they were still going to the game. Malik rushed to get his self together in time.

They made it by halftime.

The remainder of the game was exciting. LeBron James didn't disappoint, nor did Dwight Howard. LeBron gave Orlando

30 and 10 in a winning effort in overtime. Howard had 22 points and 20 rebounds, but couldn't get it done.

Malik could see Melissa enjoyed herself. Her smile gave her away. She couldn't stop. His attraction was instant, not just physical. Malik was feeling her vibe. He wanted to go to the Flats, the main kick it spot in Cleveland, but Melissa had to work. Malik did too, but he didn't care.

On the ride home they talked about relationships. They discussed everything that came to mind, giving each other a quick feel for the other. Somehow, they both just wanted the other to know they were serious about their craft, serious about achieving success, serious about the person they're serious about.

Malik pulled up at Melissa's apartment.

"You have a good time?" asked Malik.

"I did."

"Why you always smiling?" he asked.

"I didn't think it was a law against smiling," said Melissa. "And what if I can't stop smiling because of you?"

"I just asked cuz it keeps distracting me," Malik said slyly. "It's pretty sexy, and alluring. So, if you say it's because of me, I would say—I love the way you stroke my ego."

She smiled even wider and looked out the window realizing she was already falling for the guy.

"I've never went on a date with a complete stranger before," she claimed. "I at least get to know them over the phone or something. Never this fast. Never to another city. I was a little nervous but now I'm thinking it was a good decision."

Melissa waited in silence for Malik to respond. Malik thought before he spoke, so she waited a minute.

"I know what you mean," he said, after the long pause. "I think the change of pace made you nervous. Not knowing if I was the person you thought I was made you even more nervous. Tonight just made you question your own judgment."

"What are you?" she asked. "A psychiatrist or a barber?"

And a D-boy ...

"Hold on," Malik said as he held up a finger. "I'm not finished. I don't want you to think I'm scheming or tryna manipulate your feelings, cuz I'm not. Everything I say and do is genuine. No games, no gimmicks."

Melissa put her finger on his lips, leaned forward, and kissed him. It was slow, and intentional. Wet and passionate. She felt her body heat rise when their lips touched. A pool of moisture freed itself from within when their tongues met. Melissa quickly pulled away, opened the door, and jumped out of the truck. Malik could only watch with confusion. His phone rang.

"Hello?"

"I'm sorry," began Melissa. "You're so … like … I'm into you right, but you have this quality about you—I don't know what it is, but it's just something about you that I can't put my finger on. Maybe I just need more time to get to know you, but as of right now you got me movin' waaayyy too fast. I had to leave. Hopefully, I can get me at least one more date."

She hung up without another word.

*

"God thank you for allowing me to make it home tonight. Thank you for allowing me my freedom. Thank you for all of your many blessings. I ask that you don't abandon me Lord, I ask that you continue to walk with me and shine your light on me. I know what I do is not conducive to your teachings Father, but I'm trying, and I beg for your forgiveness, and your help. Please continue to bless my family, my daughter, and really the whole nation. We all need you. In Jesus name I pray, Amen."

CHAPTER 2

L was one of Malik's best friends. They've known each other since high school. The two used to come into school smelling like a field of marijuana, leaving an aroma in each and every hallway they graced. At the time, both, L and Malik were simply advertising their product. Malik walked around school with his book bag on his back with sacks of weed in every compartment. L simply kept his coat on and pitched sacks to his fellow students while the teacher wrote on the blackboard. It was funny. Their friendship was solidified years later when Malik helped L in a winless brawl because L ran his mouth in the wrong neighborhood.

L thought of those days as he was smoking a cigarillo to himself playing Madden 09' online. Malik was on his way to pick up L to go to the liquor store. L pressed pause on the game and opened the bag full of pills, he broke one in half, suddenly, his phone rang.

"You outside?" asked L.

"Yup," said Malik

"Here I come."

L walked outside into the damp air of April. Malik checked his homeboy's apparel.

"Okay," yelled Malik over the music. He turned it down from the steering wheel. "Artful Dodger, check. New Era, check. Nike Air, check."

"Nigga please, I know you aint talkin," L responded. "Cartier's, check. Pelle Pelle, check. Diamond bez."

"Yeah alright mufucka," Malik said. "Wut it do?"

"Tryna bite down?" L asked.

L opened his hand as Malik pulled off.

"Just a half of one," pleaded L.

"You know I don't fuck around cuz," said Malik.

L opened his mouth showing Malik he had already popped the other half.

"Fool," said Malik.

They stopped at the liquor store on Dorr and Westwood, copped a fifth of Ciroc and cigarillos. Some how, the two men damn near knew everyone in the store. Malik walked out with the liquor, and L walked out programming two University of Toledo female students into his phone. Twenty minutes they pulled up to a house on Laskey Ave.

"L, how long you known deez broads?" asked Malik.

"Nigga, do I question you when you take me somewhere," asked L. "But you know, I met deez hoes at Jalapeno's one night. They say they roommates, and the one I'm on say she like both sexes. I quit tryna figure shit out after that. Feel me?"

"Yea alright," is all Malik could say, as L entered the house first.

"What the fu ...,"said L.

"You gotta be bullshittin," said Malik.

The modest looking house transformed into an adult playground inside. The two women sat in a hot tub placed in the middle of the living room. The women's kitchen was decorated with all stainless steel Kenmore appliances. The parquet floors reminded Malik of the Boston Garden. Pots, pans, and glasses, hung from the ceiling. Malik noticed the granite counter tops that supported Remy XO, Grey Goose, Ciroc, Tanqueray Gin, margarita mix, tequila, Patron, Hennessy Paradis, and of course 151. There was a flat screen in front of the Jacuzzi, in the kitchen, and Malik swore he saw a glow from what he thought could only be the bathroom. There were a few coffee tables, a Nintendo Wii, a couple of plants, but otherwise no furniture in the living room.

"Damn," Malik said.

"Damn," said L. "What ya'll was on, Extreme Home Makeover or sumthin."

The women looked at each other.

"So L, damn, you gonna introduce us to your friend or what," said one of the ladies. "Hi, I'm Jennifer."

Malik observed Jennifer. He could tell she tanned. She had blonde hair and green eyes. Her breast looked firm.

"Not too much, not too little," he thought.

"How you doin? I'm Malik. Nice tan. Looks like honey," Malik smiled.

Jennifer smiled back.

"I'm Toni," she said.

Malik observed her dark brunette hair. Toni had a sexy haircut, sexy lips, sexy green eyes, but she was a lot paler than Jennifer. Not pasty, just not as brown. However, she was still very alluring. Her swag was an A plus. Toni's breast seemed to be larger, but as they rose out of the Jacuzzi to shake hands, Malik saw what he was waiting to see. Ass! Both Toni and Jennifer were holding. Their thighs were so well toned, so thick. Their asses were amazing. He'd never seen a white woman with so much ass ... let alone two. Black women needed to be proud that they made the world accept and adopt the curvaceous and voluptuous figure.

"Damn," said Malik.

"Man, ya'll the truth," said L.

"Are ya'll getting in the Jacuzzi?" asked Toni

"Should we?" said L.

"Ya'll should," Jennifer replied.

"Pour us a drink," L said.

"K," replied Toni. "Hey, Lamont."

"Oh, Lamont," whispered a laughing Malik. "I bet they could get that government out you boy."

"Wut up," said L.

"Did you bring em?" asked Toni.

"Fa sho," L said.

L threw the party pack on the table. Both Malik and L watched the girls scoot towards the x, noticing that neither one of them had on bikini's. They wore lingerie bra and panty sets. Toni's was black lace with thong bottoms. Jennifer wore almost the same thing in red. Malik and L couldn't believe their luck.

"Malik, you poppin," asked Jennifer.

"Naw, but you can pass me that drank doe."

Jennifer brought him the Ciroc in a tall glass. Malik took a sip.

"Damn, what's this?" asked Malik. "This shit potent as fuck,"

"It's Patron, Ciroc, and Grey Goose, mixed with cranapple and pineapple juice. Toni and I call it … ."

Jennifer started laughing.

"What's so funny?" asked L.

"You guys are gonna laugh," said Jennifer. "It's called oral sex."

Jennifer burst out into a loud laughter. She put a pill on her tongue walked over to Toni and kissed her in the mouth.

"You sure, you don't want one Malik?" asked Toni.

"I'm good."

"Are you?" asked Jennifer, looking in the direction of L.

He walked over to the girls and put one on each hip. He pulled out the other half of the pill from earlier. Toni performed the same ritual as Jennifer. Malik drank his oral sex. Jennifer walked over to Malik, took off his jacket, his shirt, and stripped him down to his boxers.

"We have a meeting in the Jacuzzi," said Jennifer as she guided Malik to the water.

L and Toni followed suit.

L noticed the bubbling water made his pill kick in in double time once the warmth from the Jacuzzi blanketed him. His mouth moved involuntarily. Malik noticed and started mimicking his friends jaw. They began to laugh. Malik was intoxicated at the moment as well. The oral sex went straight to his head. He felt different somehow. He remembered the ingredients. His head was tight. He got in Jennifer's ear sounding like a hood politician.

"Damn," he thought. "I just said some wild shit to this bitch."

He carried on.

"I'm sayin baby, I'm really digging your style, you need a nigga like me to teach you what you lack. Trust me you don't lack much, but you seem incomplete," he whispered in her ear. "I don't wanna sound like the rest of these lames claimin they gon' complete you. Let me show you I just wanna help you complete yourself. You a woman that should have no limits, and I happen to think your possibilities are endless. You can sponsor my dreams and I can make em a reality. Feel me? You might think I'm spittin game, but I don't spit game, I just speak reality."

Jennifer thought he sounded like a pimp, but he said everything so fast and smooth, he sounded so genuine. She didn't know whether it was the x or him that had her wetter than the Jacuzzi already did. Jennifer reached down in the water and grabbed his already erect penis.

"Whoa," she blurted out.

Jennifer kissed Malik in the mouth. Normally he didn't kiss in the mouth. He thought it was strange he permitted it.

"Come with me," whispered Jennifer.

Malik followed her to a back room. It was a sunroom with tinted windows. He could see the backyard, and the side street next to it, but no one could see them. Jennifer slipped out of her wet garments, dropped to her knees, and freed Malik's lust.

"Would you like some more oral sex," she laughed.

CHAPTER 3

Melissa thought about Malik often. She adored the
man. Two months ago when she'd met him, she knew it was
something about him that she just couldn't figure out, but she
loved that about him. Still it was *that* something that kept her
wondering. She knew he owned a barbershop. She knew he
cut hair as well. She knew the shop did well, but she also knew
it wasn't a money machine. Somehow Malik continued to bless
her with gift after gift. She questioned what he could afford.

Then there was this unspoken respect everyone had for
him. It wasn't that they were scared of him or intimidated, just
respectful. She'd never known a man like him. Every time she'd
meet one of his friends its always, "that's the man right there,"
or "how can I be like you," or the notorious, "if I had your hands
I would cut mine off."

Melissa didn't understand it. He was just a barber. She
thought he may have sold drugs. She'd even asked him once.

"You see me go to work every day, work out in the
evening, and chill at night. When exactly would I have time to
do this," he asked.

But he never said no.

She let it go because it made sense to a degree. The
truth was, though he usually did those things on schedule, but
sometimes he wouldn't be at the gym, sometimes he would be
out all night. However, he always made time for her. Why
complain?

As Melissa sat in her apartment, she realized she'd only talked to Malik once, earlier in the day when he brought her lunch. He hadn't called to talk shit like he normally did. She thought it to be odd. Melissa decided to call. She scrolled through her phone stopping at the name Future in her smart phone.

She pressed send.

Melissa quickly hung up before Malik's phone rang.

"I don't wanna be like every other woman he's come across though," she spoke out loud. "Insecure putting their man in a situation he aint even in. I'll just text him."

Damn not thinkin bout me 2 day?

*

L heard the chime coming from Malik's phone. It was 1:30 a.m. There was no doubt it was Melissa. He checked it himself. To no surprise of his, it was "Future."

Toni was changing the c.d.

"Malik, your Future calling," said L.

Malik flinched at the thought of his woman, as if she were standing in the doorway. He felt immediate guilt. The guilt turned into a conflicting emotion of pleasure. Jennifer was squeezing her secret muscles around his sex, producing an endless stream of wetness. They had been grinding for an hour straight. Jennifer cried out multiple orgasms, but Malik didn't even feel close to one. She slid back and forth on his erection as he pounded her from the back. Malik grabbed her hips pulling her backwards forcing her to take every inch.

"Oh my God," said Jennifer exhausted and out of breath. "I think I'm coming again. Oooh shi—shit, right there—harder baby, fuuuuuuck—I'm doing it again."

Jennifer's body shook as if she was having a seizure. A wave of pleasure flushed out of her body. Suddenly, Malik's muscles tightened. His whole body tensed. He continued to thrust inside of Melissa harder and harder until he came to an abrupt halt.

"Oh shiiit, ooooh shit, shit, shit," muttered Malik as he faked his orgasm.

Jennifer smiled so hard her face hurt.

"I'm gonna go wash up real quick," Malik said.

"Towels in the closet next to the bathroom, second door on the left," said Jennifer. "Did he just fuck me into loving him? Holy shit."

"Aye, L, where my ph--."

L was engaged in an act Malik couldn't describe. It looked familiar, but the acrobatics were different. Malik watched for a minute, smiling at his friend literally screwing Toni backwards.

"Right there by the drank my nigga," answered L not missing a stroke.

Malik grabbed his phone laughing towards the bathroom.

"Damn, a screen in here too?" he asked himself, texting at the same time.

Always thinkin bout you! Wildin wit this nigga L.

Ten seconds later Future text him back.

Melissa: Thought you were ignoring me.

Malik: Never dat. Couldn't hear...sup?

Melissa: Just thinkin bout u, missed u.

Malik: Is that so. Good or bad?

Melissa: Both.

Malik: Oh,am I in trouble. Lol!

Melissa: Don't laugh, u might be.

Malik: Whatever chump I'm a call when I leave.

Melissa: Don't forget.

Malik: I won't.

Melissa: Muah!

"Easy enough," L thought. "Now what am I going to do with this white bitch?"

Malik was usually a night owl, but he felt extra energized for some reason. Cool, "player" he thought. Then he remembered the lines he spit in Jennifer's ear. Then he thought about all of the adjectives his friends used to describe how they felt off x.

"I know this bitch didn't," Malik said aloud.

"Aye man," Malik started to ask but his train of thought was knocked off its tracks when he walked in on Jennifer touching herself.

She wasn't masturbating, in the traditional sense. She just laid on the cushioned wicker chair. Jennifer caressed her body. Eyes closed making the sounds of sex. She must've felt Malik's presence, because she opened her eyes.

"Damn, I'm rolling so hard," said Jennifer. "Your body looks like an art sculpture, and your dick—damn your dick should be considered a weapon. You want me to do something with that?"

Malik stood there watching her. He looked down at himself, noticing he was standing at full attention the whole time. Before he got the chance to answer, Jennifer was back on him, trying to take all of him into her mouth. Malik's eyes rolled into the back of his head.

"Fuck it then," Malik said.

CHAPTER 4

"Let me get five hundred on Cleveland then lame," said Tony.

"Naw nigga you gotta give me some points or something," said Pook.

Pook and Tony gambled against each other all of the time.

"Alright, dig," said Tony. "Gimme Cleveland over Memphis and I'll take—who da Lakers play?"

"Da Clippers," said Pook.

"Fuck it, I'll take the Clippers. The same way doe, no points, straight up," said Tony.

"Bet it then nigga," said Pook.

"It's on," said Tony as he hung up the phone.

He called Malik.

"Hello," said Malik.

"I see you at it early," said Tony.

"Boy oh boy I aint even been to sleep," said Malik.

"Where you at?"

"Da shop," Malik replied.

"What happened?" Tony asked. "It was rockin' that hard?"

"My nigga, it was just crazy I'm a have to fill you in later," said Malik. "I got customers right now but I think this broad hit me with a threx bomb."

"Wut?"

"Yeah bro you know it's a wild one fa sho, but fu-get all dat ...," Malik tried to cover up his curse word.

"Dolla jar," somebody yelled from the depths of the barbershop.

Malik pulled a dollar bill out of the same jeans he had on the day before.

"What's good doe," asked Malik.

"Shit you know it's Saturday," said Tony. "You know seeing if you fuckin wit a boss tonight, or what."

"Nigga you swear you dat deal," Malik said. "But fa real I lightweight played baby girl last night. I feel bad. Shit got too blatant. So, I'm prolly gonna be kissing ass tonight. You know I love her."

Tony laughed at his friends' admission.

"Aint nuttin wrong wit dat," Tony said. "Hit me up, let me know."

"It's on," said Malik.

Twenty minutes later Tony pulled up to Ruby's Soul Food restaurant. He hopped out of his blue Chevy Tahoe, wearing a white Jockey V-neck underneath a blue and white wool Pelle jacket, and light blue Pelle jeans. Tony reached down and wiped a spec off his white Creative Recreations. Tony met his cousin inside.

"Cuzzo," said Tony.

"What's good," said Sean. "You wanted that salmon and rice right?"

"Whatever, it don't matter cuz that's what I ordered," Tony replied.

Sean was as dark as Dikembe Mutombo. He wore a red Houston Texans hat over his fresh waves. His spiritless black eyes were menacing. Sean definitely had a story to tell. His white thermal hugged a stocky frame. Sean also wore light blue jeans but with white Air Force Ones.

He was an average looking man, with the whitest teeth ever. He knew his smile was blinding so he always tried to use it to his benefit. It was a disarming trait after staring into his eyes. The food arrived.

"Pass me that hot sauce," said Sean pouring a half of bottle on three pieces of catfish. "Check dig doe."

"Wut up?" said Tony.

"You know I got love fo ya boy, cuz you know—that's yo nigga. He hold you down and vice versa, right," said Sean.

"You already know the deal, nigga why you actin brand new," Tony asked. "What up?"

"Look man apparently this nigga Malik fuckin somebody broad or ex broad or sumthin," said Sean.

"How you know?" asked Tony. "And he stay in a nigga bitch. That aint news."

"No doubt, but—I guess this particular nigga don't wanna let the hoe go. On some typical hoe shit," said Sean. "Talkin bout he gon' fuck Malik up when he see him and all dat."

"What nigga?" asked Tony.

"Some nigga named Roscoe," Sean said.

"Roscoe from where?"

"I guess the nigga just got out," Sean said. "He did like an eight ball or sumthin. Think he shot some nigga tryna rob him a while back."

"Oh, you talkin bout fat Roscoe," Tony shot back. "Be on the North?"

"Yeah, only the nigga cut up like a bad bag of dope right now. That fat shit out the door," said Sean. "Anyway, I guess he heard Malik been gettin that gwap, so I suppose he tryna kill two birds with one stone. He asked my man if he tryna get down on this murder lick."

"Murder lick—oh yea," asked Tony.

He didn't like anybody fucking with Malik. Malik was in the life true enough. And on more than one occasion Malik proved he could handle himself. But Malik wasn't like that. Malik would rather get money, heave sex, and stay away from the beef. Malik never inflicted harm on anybody that didn't deserve it. Still, Malik was no coward. Tony knew once he told Malik, Malik's mind would go into overdrive, and he would start thinking strategically immediately.

"Who is the bitch bro?" Tony asked.

"See that's the only problem the person who told me don't know the bitch," Sean said.

"Well how dude find out Malik was hittin' her?" asked Tony.

"Oh that was simple, he found Malik's card in her bedroom."

"So, when I tell him he gotta think about every mother and bitch wit a taper that he gave his card to?" Tony asked. "That's wack, but Roscoe shoulda stayed his ass in the joint. I aint never seen a pull up that can stop these ones. Let's bounce."

Later that evening Malik had a lot on his mind when he picked up Melissa. All he could think about was the lame that was trying to take his life over a woman he probably didn't even deal with. Then it occurred to Malik as he looked over at

Melissa. It could be her. He looked Melissa over. She was beautiful. She was quietly singing along to The Dream's song, "Purple Kisses." He got weak at the sight of her Mac glossed lips, her smooth caramel complexion, her beautiful light brown eyes, and her long eyelashes. She wore a simple black blouse and black BCBG jeans, hugging her hips tight. The warm April night allowed her to wear a pair of open toed black pumps — which Malik thought made her walk like a model.

Malik processed his thoughts. He realized if Melissa made him feel how he did in three months, he could only imagine how a brother with less polish would act. Malik pulled into the parking lot of the Navy Bistro.

Melissa noticed they hadn't had much conversation on the way to the Bistro. She wondered what was bothering him. Somehow, he seemed unapproachable. Malik was usually in high spirits. They were escorted to their table and sat.

"Can I get you guys anything to drink?" the waiter inquired.

"Yeah, let me get the strongest margarita ya'll got," Malik said.

"Hmm," the waiter chuckled. "And ma'am?"

"I'll just have a little wimpy one."

"Not a problem, I shall return," the waiter said.

"Baby, what's wrong?" asked a concerned Melissa. Her face looking as perfect as it has ever looked.

"Nothing," Malik answered.

She smacked her lips to his reply.

"Stop lyin'," she told him. "I know when you got stuff on your mind. Boy you aint foolin nobody."

"Okay well look," Malik said. "Let me ask you something."

The waiter interrupted him.

"Here you go, strong and wimpy," the waiter said. "Have you decided on any appetizers or a main course?"

Malik looked at the waiter's nameplate.

"Naw, could you give us a couple of minutes please?" Malik asked.

"Oh, I'm sorry. I'm Larry, yes certainly a few minutes," the waiter said as he walked away.

Malik continued, "You been keeping it funky?"

"What?" Melissa asked, apparently caught off guard by Malik's question.

She'd thought it was his daughter, or the shop, or something about Tony. She wondered where he was going, and if it was in the direction that she thought.

"Oh, you don't know what that mean?" Malik said calm, but yet serious. "You don't talk much about your past relationships. I mean, you know about mine. At least the ones that counted. But you ... I don't know what's been going on. So, why don't you fill me in?"

Melissa blew out a breath. She did have a secret. It was something that she held from Malik. It wasn't to be sneaky, but she just didn't think it mattered.

"Okay, well that's a reasonable request," said Melissa. "But you seem so disturbed, upset even, I don't wanna piss you off."

"Damn it's like that," Malik said. "Is it that bad?"

"No," she said. "Well, not really. I never told you because I didn't think it mattered."

"Hello again," Larry the waiter intervened. "Ready?"

"Yeah, let me get the crab cakes as an appetizer," said Malik. "And let me get this broiled salmon, Caesar salad, with bleu cheese."

"And I'll have the New England Lobster," said Melissa. "With everything he ordered, except may I have raspberry vinaigrette?"

"Yes ma'am," said Larry. "I'll be back with your crab cakes."

"I'm listenin," said Malik. "You aint think it mattered."

"I didn't because he chose to do some unnecessary things that I told him not to do in the first place," said Melissa. "So, when he did what he did, it was over with for me. I was young, but I know I aint want nobody that would attempt to kill someone over a false sense of security."

Malik was debating on whether or not to tell her what he was told. He also wanted to know what the nigga was doing over her house.

"So, what was this nigga doin over your house?" Malik was frustrated.

He felt like he was slipping because he really cared.

"My house?" questioned Melissa. "He was never at my house. He just showed up out of nowhere. He came to my mom's house."

Melissa paused as if she just had a revelation.

"How did you know about all of this?"

"Crab cakes?" Larry placed three palm sized crab cakes in front of the couple. "Your dinner should be around shortly. Would you like anything else, more drinks?"

"We're fine for now," said Melissa. "I'm listenin."

Melissa smiled her beautiful Colgate smile exposing those deep dimples Malik couldn't resist.

"I know everything," said Malik.

"You know what," she began. "Normally I wouldn't be satisfied with that answer. But since you put it that way ... let me ask you what secrets you got in your closet. How *do you know everything, sir?"*

Malik cut a piece of crab cake and shoved it in Melissa's mouth.

"Let's eat," said Malik. "I'm a barber. I hear things."

"Mmmhmm, that's good. Here, taste," said Melissa, as she returned the favor. "I'm serious Malik. Something isn't right about you. I know you got some things going on that I don't know about. I mean my ex is just that, my ex. I'm over it, he's not. I want you and you only. But I've been around you long enough to know about your looks that say don't ask, about your mysterious meetings, about money—dude, you don't cut that much hair."

"Okay well this aint the place for that kind of conversation," Malik said. "I'll tell you what you want to know, but it was my past. This is Toledo. It's bound to come out anyway."

"Dinner is served," Larry interrupted. "Lobster for the lady, and broiled salmon for the gentleman."

They ate, laughed, drank, and left. On the way home Malik told Melissa about his past. All his jail time, his life involving drugs, but he didn't tell her that he still played around a little. He told her that he still had money put up from past ventures. He decided not to mention Roscoe's plans. He figured he'd deal with that another way. They spent the night together. Luckily, Melissa was going through her cycle. Malik was exhausted. As soon as his face hit the pillow, he fell asleep.

*

While Malik was asleep, Tony was plotting. Nothing like the element of surprise, he thought. Tony and Sean sat in the Norwich Apartments awaiting their prey. The maroon Oldsmobile Nine-Eight blended in perfectly next to the dumpster. Both Sean and Tony wore dark blue hoody's and Under Armour gloves. They sat in silence as they released the safety off of their throw away Bryco nine millimeter pistols. They both checked the clips and pulled back the hammer.

"Get out," said Sean.

A white 2002 Pontiac Grand Prix pulled in the parking lot.

"Yup that's him," said Tony, as he stepped out of the vehicle. He went to hide behind a dumpster.

The Grand Prix parked four cars away. Tony pulled his hood over his head, crouching like a wide receiver about to run a route. His target got out. Tony knew he had to be careful because he wasn't on his blind side. Tony tucked his hands and pistol inside his hoody pocket.

"Aye, my nigga," said Tony.

His prey turned around.

45

"Wut up. Who dat?"

"Dis Trip my nigga," said Tony.

"Who?" the target asked.

All the while, Tony was moving closer.

"Trip," said Tony. "I'm looking for Michelle. You know where she stay?"

"Michelle who?" asked the target. "Michelle, in this building?"

One step … two … three.

"Yeah, she told me to come through," said Tony. "Now she aint answering the phone."

Four steps … five.

"Oh yea," the target stepped down and grabbed his phone. "You said your name is what?"

Six … seven.

"Trip, cuz your ass is slippin," said Tony as he pulled out the Bryco.

Pop! Pop! Pop!

Rod fell back into the doorway with three holes in his abdomen. Tony walked up looking into Rod's solemn face.

"Lost one," said Tony.

Rod began to plea for his life.

Pop!

Tony ran to the car. Sean pulled off, turning down Norwich. He calmly crossed Reynolds road into a residential area. Sean made a series of turns until he came out onto Airport Highway. Sean turned right, then right again in between Bally's Fitness Club and a Sprint dealership. He came to a curve, pulled out of sight of the heavy traffic. Tony got out, wiped off the weapons, broke them down and buried them as an extra precaution. The duo then walked down the street and hopped into a black Chevy Avalanche. Tony jumped in the driver seat. They tossed the hoody's in the back, turned on the radio, and drove off.

47

CHAPTER 5

Malik had a strange relationship with his daughter's mother. Well maybe not strange, but definitely different. They weren't a couple, yet they communicated with each other with the efficiency of a long time husband and wife. Malik didn't believe in drama with any of his female companions, past or present. To him it was a waste of energy. He knew it always boiled down to somebody still having feelings for the other and he played off that. His charm and politeness disarmed many of the women he dealt with. Malik always addressed women with respect, not always deserving.

Malik didn't think he was God's gift to women. He just knew if one could understand a particular woman's thought process the rest was relatively easy. He knew he wasn't ugly. He had money in the bank. He had his own business, car, and home. At twenty-eight he finally had his first child. Malik knew the ugliest man, accompanied by those accomplishments would have to beat at least a couple of women away with a stick. Malik knew the difference between surface traits and traits that were part of a person's core, which is why his personality was award winning.

Inez, Malik's daughter's mom, was one that wished she could enjoy Malik's personality as she once did. She'd made some bad decisions while they were together, which is why the two parents weren't together. Inez was Arabic and white. She had long black hair that stretched down to her ass. She had beautiful brown eyes, thick lips and an appealing smile. Inez stood about five foot-three, a hundred and thirty pounds. She was extremely attractive. The main thing that won Malik over was the way she was down for her nigga ... and off course her body didn't hurt at all. She was built to say the least.

"Wut up?'

"You daddy," Inez said. "Say hi to daddy."

Inez grabbed Dejanique's little hand and waved at Malik. Malik walked over and picked up Dejanique from Inez's arms. He never talked to his daughter in baby talk. He always talked to her as if she was an adult that could talk back.

"Who put these clothes on you," asked Malik as if Dejanique would tell him.

"Boy gone," said Inez. "Why you always talking shit, and why you always talking like she can talk back."

"So she can pick shit up quicker Inez. What make you think she understand all that googy ga ga shit. What does that mean?" asked Malik. "One day I'm gon' ask her some shit and she gon' be like 'mama did that hoe ass shit daddy,' watch."

They laughed at that one.

"So when you coming to pick mommy up?" asked Inez.

"When mommy gets her head out of her ass and get off that bullshit she's on," Malik said. "When mommy figure out it's only one Malik Hawkins round this muthafucka."

"I'm gon' surprise you one day, watch," said Inez. "We gon' be one big happy family once I get you to share that dick so I can give you your son. I know you want one."

"How you know I aint workin on that with somebody else already," said Malik.

"Ooh, I'd be crushed. Please don't do that," said Inez thinking she couldn't blame anyone but herself.

"What you still fuckin with that Melissa chick?"

"Mmmhmm," Malik answered.

"She's cute, but do she got this top of the line?"

Inez spread her thighs slightly to give Malik a visual.

"You tore up dude," said Malik. "Dejanique, let's ride."

Inez waited for Malik to grab all of Deja's things. She stopped in front him at the door, then kissed him.

"Girl you crazy," said Malik.

She grabbed at the bulge forming in his pants.

"Maybe, but I see you still like that shit, huh daddy?"

Malik laughed on his way out.

After, he piled in the toys and diaper bag, and strapped Deja in. Malik wondered why he needed all that stuff when he had it at his apartment.

"Deja I hope you don't be mad at me when you get older," Malik said. "Your mama cool, she just wasn't ready for the way your daddy handled things. But you gon' be smart enough to understand when you get older. You gonna have more polish than Windex baby. Trust me. I'ma lace ya."

Malik went on with her like that for the next two days. They watched television. He talked, she listened. Her brown almond shaped eyes stared at him every time he spoke, as if she knew exactly what he was saying. Sometimes he stared at her forehead and eyebrows and nose that were all traits that belonged to him. The rest of her features belonged to her mama. She was truly beautiful. She was his heart.

*

Toni lay in her bed fantasizing about Malik. She'd only seen him once after the festivities at her house. He seemed solid to her. His conversation was worldly and his demeanor was hood. She loved being with L, the sex was great, he was humorous, and funny. L was mentally sharp too, but that was it. She didn't think L took her seriously. Their relationship was built on partying and sex. There was no depth. She needed depth. Malik seemed to be a different breed. Her sister filled in the other blanks. Her mind wandered to the blanks she could only imagine.

Toni wondered if her sister would be upset if she, at the very least had sex with Malik. After all, they'd shared men before. Not often, but it has happened. None had the potential Malik had. *How would my sister act,* thought Toni.

Matter of the heart, or battle of the hormones?

*

Jennifer sat in her basement on her cognac colored, micro-fiber sectional. She wore blue shorts with pink written across the back, and a blue tank top with the numbers sixty-nine printed on it. She sat on the couch with the balls of her feet tucked underneath her butt. One hand holding the remote, the other hand played with her newly pedicured toes. Flicking through the channels she stopped on thirteen.

"Roderick Johnson, age twenty three, was shot just inside the door-way in the Norwich apartments. Witnesses say they heard the shots, but no one could identify the shooters,"

51

said the reporter. "I've talked to several residents in this building, and I've been told the murder took place between 2 and 2:30 a.m. early Sunday morning. Police say if you have any information that could lead to the arrest of this suspect or suspects, they urge you to call Crimestopper at 419-555-1111. I'm Sashem Brey for 13 Action News, back to you Kristian."

"Aww," Jennifer said out loud.

Jennifer thought back to a week ago when she met Malik. How she'd known at the sight of him she would be having sex with him later that evening. Since then, Jennifer had a long conversation with Malik. She learned about his daughter. She could hear her in the background making baby noises. She swore the little girl was trying to talk to her father. Jennifer had learned about Melissa. The way he talked about her, she knew her competition was stiff. Besides, Malik made it clear that she screwed up.

"Do you cheat on all your women," Jennifer recalled their conversation. "Cuz you fucked me like you didn't want me to ever go anywhere."

"Maybe I did. I might do it again," said Malik.

She smiled at the thought.

"But then again I don't cheat on all my women," said Malik. "Shit, I aint had many that I would call mine. I don't usually kiss in the mouth. I don't usually fuck for hours at a time either."

"You came at least twice," said Jennifer.

"Nope I faked one cuz Melissa was calling, which is when I came to the realization that something wasn't right.

Now I aint all the way mad at you, cuz I prolly would've fucked you either way," he said. "But you disappointed me when I realized you put a illy in my drink."

"I am so sorry," she said. "I thought you popped. When you said you didn't, I didn't want to look like a "date raper," so I just brought you the drink. I didn't think you would notice."

"What if I had a bad reaction? What if I woulda dropped a dirty for my probation officer," asked Malik. "Yo ass aint factor in that shit, huh?"

Jennifer remembered feeling like scum. She tried to apologize, offered to make it up to him in any way he liked, but Malik didn't budge. She had to regain his trust. He'd admitted she had potential. That was all the assurance Jennifer needed. Jennifer came to the conclusion that she had to show Malik she was a better woman for him than Melissa.

Something bothered Jennifer. It was Toni, her sister and best friend. They were only stepsisters, and only became such in high school. Their parents married when they both were sixteen. They were only twenty-six now. Jennifer remembered telling Toni about Malik. She mainly told her about the sex, but about everything else as well. She recalled Toni's eyes. They were curious and hungry. Jennifer laughed at her own insecurities. If she couldn't have Malik to herself, she would settle for him being her boy toy.

*

"Go around back. I'm a kick the front door in. They prolly gon' run out the back. That's when you put that thang to they face and walk 'em right back in."

Two men conspired to rob a dope house a few feet from where they were standing. Spring was in the air and their disguises were conducive to the weather. Black Levis, black Columbia boots, and gray and black Bathing Ape hoodies was the attire for the evening. Blue bandanas covered their mouths while sunglasses took care of the rest of their face. One man crept to the back.

*

"Nigga you can't fuck with me in this shit," said Dirty.

Dirty was nineteen years old trying out the dope game. So far, so good. All he did was sit in a house all day provided by his older brother. He played video games, swung the back door back and forth and collected money. He and Mac stayed in that house twenty-four seven. No guns, just a PlayStation, battery acid, and dope.

"Well bet yo pack on the next game," said Mac.

Mac suddenly looked up. He thought he heard something on the porch. Everyone knew to knock once on the back door. There was no knock at all. Dirty went to the bathroom. Mac got up to look out the peek hole.

Wham!

"Oh shit," said Dirty.

He thought it was the police. The men hovering over his friend didn't look like police. *Damn I should copped that iron*, he thought. It only looked like one guy. Dirty liked his chances as he grabbed a baseball bat he'd always kept by the couch.

"Where the dope at lil' nigga," asked the jack-boy.

"Right there—next to that bucket," said Mac. "Please don't kill me man I'm only eighteen man."

"Shut up bitch, shoulda thought about that before you started playing a grown man's game."

Wack!

Dirty went upside the man's head. The jack-boy tried to turn around. He was dis-oriented.

Whack! Whack! Whack!

Dirty hit the man three more times.

"You know who trap this is nigga," asked Dirty.

The gun fell from the man's hand. It dropped on to Mac's lap. Mac gripped the .357 Magnum, stood up and pointed it at the robber.

"Bust that nigga Mac," Dirty yelled.

Mac didn't hesitate.

Boom! Boom!

Mac put one round in the jack-boy's chest and one in his head.

Boom! The back door flew open. Roscoe ran in blazing, his .45 loud enough to wake the dead. Mac shot back, Dirty fell limp on the floor. Mac had Roscoe in his sights, but he hesitated looking down at his dead friend on the floor. That's all it took. Hesitation had no place in war. You get ready and you stay ready.

Boom! Roscoe's final shot damn near took Mac's entire head off.

Roscoe's accomplice, Dirty, and Mac all lay in one heap in front of the television.

A whistle blew from the T. V.

"Five second violation."

Roscoe panicked. He tried to look for the money and the dope. He got too nervous when he couldn't find it in his first couple attempts. He ran out the same way he came. Once Roscoe reached the car he started it quickly and pulled off.

"Fuck, fuuuuuuuuck, fuck! Muthafuckin little niggas. Fuuuck! My fault Tone, damn my nigga. Fuck! Shit I gotta—I gotta get the fuck outta here."

Roscoe drove to the expressway. He fled the scene with no money, no drugs, and no hostages. Roscoe had more blood on his hands than he wanted.

"Shoulda been that bitch ass nigga," Roscoe mumbled to no one in particular.

CHAPTER 6

Malik was on the other side of town taking care of some business of his own.

"Thirteen what?" asked Malik.

"Come on Malik," said Juan. "You know what it is, it's ruff out here."

"Yea I know, I'm sayin doe, last month it was one thing and you like, it's going to be sweet for a while. A month aint a while, my nig. Feel me?" said Malik. "I got a nigga out west been tryna fuck with me. You're fluctuating like the Dow homie."

"Bro, you know if I had another play I would make it," said Juan. "But, as it is, this is what I'm working with."

Juan was a close friend of Malik's. They didn't kick it much due to the business at hand. They exchanged gifts at Christmas, and partied out of town, but indictments were tricky. The best that either of them could do was minimize their exposure together. It wasn't the fact that they were heavy weight kingpins, because they weren't. However, cases have been built on less than what they were doing. They felt like they were better off staying more safe than sorry. They both had years in the penitentiary. No one was trying go back.

Malik studied Juan's' features. He had small brown eyes, African dark skin, and a razor lined Rick Ross beard. Juan's wrinkled forehead rose into a freshly shaven baldhead. His ears twinkled like the night sky from the 4 ct. diamond earrings in each ear, which contrasted with the rest of his average apparel, which included a blue t-shirt and blue sweatpants.

"You know you bustin me right?" asked Malik. "It's cool cuz I only brought eleven-five wit me."

Malik passed Juan a Havana Joe bag.

"Dirty ass nigga," said Juan. "Slanging all dat shit in the hood, broke ass nigga."

"Inflatin ass nigga."

"Short ass nigga."

"Middle man ass nigga."

"Owe me fifteen-hundred ass nigga."

"Get it like Mayweather ass nigga."

"Oh fa real," laughed Juan. "Should I make that call now summabitch?"

"Aint gon do you no good. I got at least an hour head start," said Malik. "And don't think I don't know where the rest at."

Malik pretended to use his cell phone.

"Hello? Is this Goons-R-Us?"

"Ok, ok," Juan laughed. "Quit playin all the time."

"It's all luv b. It's been real I got life on my waist," said Malik. "I'm out chea."

"Call me let me know you cool," said Juan.

"It's on," said Malik.

Malik walked out of Juan's house into the driveway and pulled off in a rented white Dodge Charger. He took every back street he could to get to Alexis. Malik picked up his phone.

"You still there?" asked Malik.

"Yes baby," said Charmaine. "Where would I go in your time of need?"

"No need for the sarcasm chump. I'm on the way."

Charmaine was a friend of Malik's. They were more like friends with benefits, but their friendship was more important than the benefits. They knew the relationship wouldn't amount too much so more often than not, they kept it cordial. Malik and Charmaine's friendship was a strange one, yet affectionate and genuine.

Twenty minutes later Malik pulled up to the Townhouse just off of Alexis Road. He opened the door, and heard the shower running.

"Charmaine," Malik yelled.

"Yeaas," she sang.

He walked into the bathroom.

"Didn't I tell you I was on the way?"

"Don't you got a key?"

"So, what! You need to be attentive around this muthafucka."

"Shut up jerk."

Malik turned on the bathroom sink, and filled up a cup of water.

"What you doin?" she asked.

Malik opened the curtain and threw cold water on her.

"Malik," she shrieked. "OOOOH I'M FUCKIN YOU UP! WATCH."

Malik laughed on his way to his tuck spot. Charmaine got out the shower and put on her lotions and fragrances. She walked downstairs to the living room in a pair of pink boxers and white tank top. She was a piece of work. She stood every bit of five feet nine inches, holding a favorable one hundred forty pounds. Her pedicure was always new. Her legs were scar less and healthy. Her butter pecan skin was smooth and unblemished. Her thighs were thick and distracting. Her hips were curvy and seductive. Her waist was trim, stomach flat, and breast were 36 c's. Her manicure was always new. Her arms were delicate. Her posture was perfect. She had lips like Megan Good's, cheekbones like Janet, and eyes like Stacy Dash. Yes, Charmaine was a winner. Most men didn't know how to keep their composure around her. That's what drew her towards Malik.

They met five years before. He wasn't paying much attention to her, and she knew she commanded it that night. Wearing a short jersey dress and stilettos, her intention was to kill the club. Just like now, here she was, smelling like a field of fruit wearing little to nothing, and this nigga watching basketball. Malik glanced at her out of the corner of his eyes, then right back to Dwayne Wade and the Miami Heat.

"How was that cold shower," asked Malik.

"F-U Malik," said Charmaine.

"Bet you aint horny no more," laughed Malik. "Iz ya?"

"Gimme my money," Charmaine stuck her hand out.

Malik twisted his lips trying to conceal his smile.

"Damn, that's what it's about huh? M.O.M."

"What's that mean?"

"Money over Malik," he answered.

She laughed.

"Boy gone. You know I'm playin. But I do needs my cash."

"Yea, it's already in your room, next to that uhhh, massager in your drawer."

Charmaine blushed, but couldn't control her smile.

"Whatever dude, its drought season 'round here. I was bout to massage myself before I was so rudely interrupted."

"Now baby you know I'll scratch that itch for you," said Malik.

"Very tempting Mr. Goodbar. I aint got no business fuckin you. Plus I like Melissa. That'd be rude."

"Naw, you don't got no business fuckin me. Although it aint like we aint never did no rude shit before. Only on your terms, I guess. I feel so used," Malik pretended to cry. "It's cool doe. I got a white bitch that go sooo hard."

"Ugh, come on then. I'll give you some just so you don't
… ."

"Sorry," Malik interrupted. "I regretfully decline. I'm
going to the Alps tonight."

"You so stupid."

"You so prejudice."

"Really I'm not. I was just playin," said Charmaine.

She walked toward where Malik sat, and straddled his
lap.

"But I wasn't just playin."

"Whoa," said Malik as Charmaine kissed him long and
hard until she felt him grow in his jeans. She kissed his neck,
suddenly his phone rang.

"Aww man," Charmaine whined.

"Hello?"

"Sup nigga," Tony sounded disturbed. "Come get me
A.S.A.P."

"You cool bro?" asked Malik.

"Naw, somebody just tried to rob my girl," said Tony.

"I'm on da way."

Malik didn't regret being the friend of all friends, but
when he looked at Charmaine's gorgeous face he regretted
having to leave.

"I gotta go."

"What happened?"

"Man stuff," said Malik, "rain check?"

"Maybe. I'm feelin you right now for some reason."

Malik smiled and left. Truth was Charmaine always felt him. But they couldn't be together, she wouldn't stress it, and that was that.

"Show, hope you come back though."

*

Malik pulled up to Tony's house. Police were everywhere. He looked around the premises. Malik spotted Rene, Tony's girl. She was speaking with a detective.

Rene was more than attractive. Malik thought she looked good enough to be on T.V. somewhere. She was a chocolate sensation. Short, but put together like Alyson Felix, the track star. She had long, silky, pretty dark hair, always styled to perfection. Deep dimples buried themselves in her creamy dark cheeks every time she smiled. However, at the moment, she was distraught. She wore a yellow sweater, with a green button up underneath, blue jeans and yellow pumps. There were no noticeable defense wounds on her face or her clothes. That was a plus, Malik thought. He walked towards her.

"Rene, you alright," asked Malik.

"Malik!" Rene hugged him, disregarding the detective questions. "I was so scared, I swear to God."

"Where—"Malik paused and lowered his voice. "Where Tony at?"

"He still outta town," Rene had a confused look on her face. Malik didn't even know Tony was out of town, but he did hear about Rod. He put two and two together.

"What you tell them," Malik pointed to a squad car.

"Just what happened."

"Did they ask if you had a boyfriend?"

"No but I think he was about to ask who I stayed with," said Rene.

"Alright, finish answering their questions. Don't say you got a boyfriend," he said. "Tell em I'm your cousin and I'm gon stay with you for the night, and get em outta here."

"Okay," after Rene followed directions she walked into the house, and met Malik in the kitchen. "Alright, what's the damn deal."

"Nothin," Malik smiled. "I just didn't want you to mention Tony's name. You know them mufuckas got a way bringing shit up at the damndest times."

"True but something's up," she said.

"How you figure that?"

"Cuz you aint even know Tony was still gone."

"I'll let him explain that," said Malik. "But, what happened?"

"Awww man Malik some big dude ran up on me when I was walking to the door. He had on one of the zip up thingies."

"What the fuck is a zip up thingie, Rene?"

"You know them ones that zip up over your whole face."

"Oh....uh...um," Malik snapped his fingers trying to remember the brand. "Skull and Bones—Bathing Ape?"

"Yea, that's it, Bathing Ape," she replied.

"And then what?" asked Malik.

"Oh he had a gun and everything. I almost pissed on myself. He told me to give him my purse and stuff, so I gave it to him," said Rene. "But then the police searched all around here and found my purse the next street over. He took my money and credit cards but my I.D. and everything was still there. Luckily he aint take my keys. I wouldn't have ever stayed here again."

"Soooo, you alright," asked Malik.

"Not really but I will be. You stayin right?" Rene frowned her face, looking like a small child.

"Yea, call Tony," said Malik. "Aye Rene, did you see his face at all?"

"Kind of, I did cuz he aint have the hood zipped all the way up he had some shades on," she said. "All I could see was he had like a scar on his nostril like somebody ripped a nose ring out of it. But that's all I remember about him."

"Dark, yellow, white?" asked Malik.

"Damn you sound like one of them annoying ass detectives. He was like brown, I guess. Not dark as you but not light as Tony neither."

"Alright, call Tony."

Rene called Tony and told him everything. She also told him how scared she was to stay by herself, and she wanted Malik to stay.

"Let me holler at Malik," said Tony.

Rene handed Malik the phone.

"Yo," said Malik.

"You cool with that—staying with her for the night?"

"I mean she kind of shook my nigga," explained Malik. "If you aint on it it's cool, but you know I figured out what's going on wit you so, you know it make sense."

"Damn you my nigga boy. It's on. I'll be back in a couple of weeks," Tony said. "Keep your eye on my baby for me. I got you."

"Man nigga I know what to do. After tonight I'm gon just tell her to stay at one of her friends' house," said Malik. "I'll keep my ears open about that other thing too. See what's really... but here's Rene."

"Baby when are you coming back," said Rene. "I miss you. I need you."

"I know baby, I'm sorry I couldn't be there for you, but Malik got you," said Tony. "If you need something don't get it from nobody else but Malik. And don't be on no bullshit. If he tell you, or suggest you do something, do it babe. That's my guy he know what's good."

"I know baby. I will. I love you."

"Love you too."

Rene knew right away something was going on. Tony didn't say when he'd be back. She knew he wasn't gone on business because he didn't make himself accessible. Rene hoped he wasn't up to anything crazy, but she knew Tony was as unpredictable as the weather.

Malik and Rene watched movies all night, took a couple shots, and played Nintendo Wii. Before they crashed out Rene thanked Malik for staying. She couldn't help but to ask Malik if everything was really okay with Tony. Malik tried to soothe her uneasiness.

"You know sometimes it's good to deviate from the regular plan, Rene," Malik said. "He's cool. This was one of those times it was better to just change clothes and go."

Rene felt a strange numbness in her veins. It was an intuition mostly mothers and wives had, that told them to brace themselves for anything. Malik hadn't promised Tony would be cool. That was enough for Rene to pray for the well being of her man. She prayed all night.

CHAPTER 7

It was a Thursday afternoon on April the seventeenth. Not a cloud cluttered the sky. The wind blew gently, and at two o'clock the temperature was at seventy. Malik, L, and Chuck were all busy cutting hair. The barbershop was full of patrons. Malik was at ease, but still couldn't help but to think about the month's events. It had been three weeks since the incident with Rene, and a little over a month since Rod was killed. Malik learned a lot of people thought Tony had something to do with it, yet there was no evidence. When Malik found out Rod was a snitch, he called Tony.

"You got a way out," said Malik. "But I heard they wanna question you. Bring a Lawyer and get down there quick so they don't think you dodging em. You got an alibi?"

"Man who you think you talkin too," said Tony." "So earlier you said he was tellin, right?"

"Yea, the nigga Drop said he set him up, and he told on Lamont when he smacked him up with the burner," Malik said. "Shit you aint the only nigga he pissed off bro."

"That's what's up."

That conversation was two days ago. Malik found out Tony went to clear his name today, but he hadn't heard anything yet. He didn't know the police made Tony sit for an hour before they began questioning him.

"You need some help," asked Malik.

Someone stood up in the waiting area.

"Happy Birthday baby," Melissa said as she walked in looking like a Goddess. She carried in an ice cream cake from Baskin Robbins and couple of balloons.

"I got your present in the car. You want me to get it?" Melissa smiled from ear to ear knowing he'd love his gifts.

"Naw, I'll wait till later," said Malik.

"Okay I wasn't asking really, I want you to have it now," said Melissa.

"Damn it must be the shit the way you smiling."

"It is."

Melissa walked to the car.

"Damn happy G-Day bro,' one patron said, they all chimed in.

"I know you gon be playin tonight with that sexy muthafucka," said L.

"And you better know it," said Malik. "The fellas can treat me on the weekend."

Melissa walked back in with two bags from Niemen Marcus.

"Hold on fam," Malik told his client.

Malik followed Melissa to the back. She pulled out a cream sweater dress by Vera Wang, brown pumps, accessorized with African inspired trinkets to coordinate the outfit. Melissa proceeded to pull out a leopard thong and bra set from Victoria

Secret. She only pulled those items up just over the top of the bag. Malik laughed.

"Okay then. What you got for daddy?"

Melissa pulled out a photo from the Victoria Secret bag and showed Malik.

"Whoa!"

She stood in the picture wearing nothing but her birthday suit. She looked like a new and improved Vanna White. Her face was smiling and her arms were stretched out, pointing to a brand new fifty-inch flat screen. The rest of Melissa's body was oiled up and shaven. Her body looked bronze, artful even. She wore some kind of heels that laced up around her calves.

Malik's mouth dropped to the floor. He was turned on instantly. He didn't even want to stay at work, he was sure to make at least another $200.

"Oh, and I found you these," Melissa pulled out a red box containing a pair of Cartier sunglasses. "I know you like these."

"Baby, you aint gone be able to walk for a week." said Malik.

*

Meanwhile, Tony was sweating it out in an interrogation room at the safety building downtown. A middle aged Hispanic detective sat across from Tony and his lawyer. The detectives name was Richard Sanchez. He was 5'11", no facial hair, chubby around the middle with dark rings under his eyes. Sanchez wore a blue tie over a white shirt and blue Dockers, worn brown shoes.

"The murder took place between 2:00 and 2:30 Atlantic Meridian, a time where most of the city is sleep."

At first Sanchez gave Tony the benefit of the doubt, before he walked in with his high priced attorney. However, he had no evidence, no eyewitness, no weapon, and Tony's alibi was righteous.

"So let me get this straight," continued Sanchez. "At the time of the murder you were where?"

"If you're correct with your time sir," Tony began. "I was just walking in the house, on a completely different side of town. It's funny because First 48 was on. That's how I know it was 2:10 exactly because my girl and her friend was up watching it, and her friend asked what time it was. I checked and she left."

"And your girls' name is?"

"Rene Timmins and her friends' name is Tichina Prescott."

"And they'll verify all of this?" asked Sanchez.

"Yup."

"One more question," Sanchez knew his lawyer wouldn't permit it but what the hell. "Why did you go out of town the next day?"

"Enough detective," Mr. Carlisle, Tony's attorney chimed in. "My client is obligated to answer questions pertaining to this case not his leisure activities. Furthermore, it seems as if you're insinuating my client knew about the murder before he left. He's not answering so, is that all?"

Sanchez rolled his eyes, and rubbed invisible crumbs off his mouth.

"I'm saying, Tony it's okay if you wanted to kill somebody who hit you over the head with a pistol," said Sanchez.

He searched Tony's face to see if it would betray him once he laid down his ace. Tony was ready for the play, he bluffed Sanchez the whole time. Tony's face held no guilt. Sanchez was unsure. Carlisle was ready for the play as well. He nodded towards Tony.

"Yeah, he smacked me over the head hard one night at the Players," said Tony. "But that was weeks ago. He also lied and said I shot at him some time after that. That turned out to be false. The fact is, your boy, may he rest in peace, lived a very dangerous life. I know of at least three other people he robbed, shot at, or snitched on. Surely your interest can't be limited with just me, Mr. Sanchez. I mean — am I the only person he offended or injured? I'm a victim and should be treated as such. Don't you think?"

Sanchez knew he was telling the truth. Rod had a record one could write a book on. Sanchez's face was stone.

"After I verify this alibi you can go," said Sanchez.

"Actually we can go now," said Carlisle. "You have no witness to say he was at the scene even if the alibi is false. Sanchez you act as if I'm not sitting here. Just clear my clients name quickly so we can go."

Tony waved good-bye to the detective got on the elevator and out the door back into freedom. Tony understood he dodged a bullet. He hopped in his truck and stared at himself in the rearview mirror. He knew he wouldn't be facing a jury, but worried about what he would say when he had to face the only judge that mattered. Tony's eyes grew sad.

"Father forgive me," Tony mumbled.

Twenty minutes later he was at the shop.

"Birthday boy," Tony yelled. "We still alive at twenty-nine, we popping bottles tonight nigga. I just saw my life flash before my eyes, and it's yo day! It goes down. What it do?

Malik walked from around his chair and gave his comrade a hug. He looked at his watch. It read, 4:45. Malik had one in the chair and two more waiting. Most of his friends didn't work on their birthdays, but Malik felt obligated to set an example since he did run the place, even though he didn't care one way or the other.

"Let me knock these two heads out the way and I'm ready," said Malik. "And how you come in here empty handed? Nigga I'll take a bottle of the finest Remy XO. Liquor store next door fool."

Tony laughed.

"You right. That's what I love about you boy," Tony said. "You never change."

Malik assessed that comment for a second as Tony walked out the door.

Is that a good thing or bad thing?

Malik shook off the thought and continued to cut. Sixty minutes later Malik was done for the day. He pulled the switch on the open sign. The light went off. Chuck and L would still cut, but of course the prices would go up. Malik poured everybody in the shop a shot of the XO Tony bought. There were seven people.

"To me my niggas, I dun came a long way and a couple of ya'll been there for most of that shit. Shit we all came a long way," said Malik. "I'm livin man. We breakin bread and that's what's up. So ... here's to coming a long way, and to going much, much further."

Everyone had their cups raised, and yelled "salud."

*

Tony followed Malik to his house. Malik explained to Tony he was going out with Melissa. He suggested Tony and Rene come join them. Tony declined, explaining how he needed to spend some time with his girl too. Tony and Malik sat around and polished off the bottle of XO. Tony could tell Malik had something on his mind.

"So what's up Malik," said Tony. "Seem like you been thinkin bout sumthin since I been wit you."

Malik looked around at his home. It wasn't an million dollar estate. He didn't have all of the things that he wished he had. Malik considered himself materialistic because he enjoyed having nice things, but he also knew that his materials didn't define him as a person. However, Malik didn't lack much at all. He did what he wanted, vacationed when he wanted, bought his daughter what she needed, and took care of his home and business accordingly. He had no complaints, he merely wanted to elevate himself to the next level.

"Bro," Malik paused. "We can't do what we doing forever man."

Tony looked at Malik confused and intoxicated. He wanted to speak but he decided not to. He felt the same way. Tony always wondered what his life would be like minus the grind. He wanted to hear what his friend had to say.

"You know when I was locked up my nigga—I prayed to God a lot. You know I aint never been a religious type nigga, but I got to thinkin. For me to continue to go back and forth to jail, never caught with any real weight, it dawned on me bro. I'm here for a reason bro," Malik said. "I don't know what the fuck it is, but that's how I'm looking at shit right now. Aint no other way to explain it.

"I'm still alive," he continued. "Shit, you and me both could just as well be in a casket somewhere kickin' it with the dead homies. Feel me? Anyway, I made a promise to God, that if he allowed me to keep the things I've acquired in order to slow down—to stop me from selling dope, to get me home to my daughter before she could walk and talk bro, I told him I'm gon give myself to him."

Tony was silent. He zoned out staring at nothing in particular.

"I know it's gon be rough for me, but I aint getting no younger man, and fa real, fa real, aint too many more niggas getting rich off the game no more. Feel me?" Malik said. "I've been reading the Qur'an and the Bible. I don't know who's right or who's wrong but I do know that they agree on two things: There is a God and there is a Heaven, and I wanna see both.

"I aint sayin I'm gonna become a deacon and all that, but just more conscious," he said. "God know aint none of us perfect, and sin is sin, but a nigga can be forgiven. When you ready, all you gotta do is ask for forgiveness for your sins. Open your heart to him and recognize Jesus as the son, know that there is only one God and nothing is greater than he and you won't lose."

"You sound like you already joined the congregation my nigga," said Tony, wiping his face.

"Naw, I've just been doin my homework," Malik countered. "I'm telling you because I plan to tell everyone I got love for—I want ya'll there with me."

"You just put a hell of a lot on my head bro," Tony said. "That was the realist shit you ever spoke."

Malik smiled.

"Maannn, I just wanted to share that wit you," said Malik. "On another note I gotta catch one more play. See how the devil work?"

Tony laughed, right before he said, "I do."

"My dude say he got a nice pack comin through sometime next month," Malik said. "What you tryna do?"

"What? Nigga, what am I tryna do? Iz you high or dumb, and I aint gon say you dumb," Tony said.

"Alright, I'm gon fill you in but you know he frontin the whole pack," Malik said. "So I'm tryna hit dude off right back A.S.A.P. No games no gimmicks. Get him out my hair and keep pushin."

"That's what it do," said Tony. "I'm a get outta here and let you get dressed. You just put a whole lot on a nigga head bro. We on for tomorrow or what?"

"Fa sho."

Tony gave Malik a hug.

"I needed to hear that shit you told me too," Tony said. "Happy G-day boy."

Malik got in the shower and got dressed. His buzzer rang just as he was spraying on his Ov Jean Paul cologne. Malik looked himself over in the mirror. His brown and maroon button up fit just right over his stocky frame. Malik rolled up the sleeves to expose the diamond bezel on his watch. He buttoned and zipped the crispy dark blue jeans he wore with brown stitching. After he tied up his maroon and brown Gucci sneakers, he finally slid on his Cartier frames Melissa bought him. The buzzer rang.

"Who is it?"

"Boy if you don't let me in," said Melissa.

Melissa walked in looking like America's Next Top Model. Her sweater dress clung to her body as if it was her second skin. The bra she wore made her breasts look as if they were drawn on. Her backside curved around underneath her dress leaving the imagination to go berserk. The heels Malik saw earlier made her stand a couple inches over his stocky frame. Melissa's face looked like an Egyptian queen. The bronze foundation blended uniquely into her unblemished epidermis. Her skin tone coordinated perfectly with her wooden African accessories.

"Boy close your mouth," said Melissa. "You should be used to your eye candy. That's why you call me future." Melissa secretly enjoyed his reaction and never got tired of it. She turned around and looked back at Malik, winking, and giving him her million-dollar smile.

"Good lawd," said Malik.

"You ready silly?"

"Oh Yeah?"

The couple started at Bravo's, a restaurant outside of the Westfield Mall. They ate, drank even danced a little. Malik and Melissa wound up at My Brother's Place dancing to every song, rubbing each other's body as if for the first time. Malik and Melissa drank shots of Patron Platinum, and shared a bottle of Dom Perignon. Melissa eventually excused herself to the bathroom. Malik decided to do the same. He barely pulled himself out of his jeans before someone walked up on him.

"Hi Malik," the stranger said.

Malik tilted his head towards the voice still doing his business.

"Toni?" Malik was unsure.

He was a little drunk.

"Yup, I know you're with your girlfriend. I see why you won't leave her. She's phenomenal," Toni said. "You should bring her to play sometime."

"Cute," said Malik.

He washed his hands.

"What you doing in here?"

"Oh I almost forgot what I wanted to tell you," she continued. "You have no idea how you distract my thoughts."

Malik's eyebrows were raised, while others began to pile into the bathroom one-by-one.

"What you talking about?"

"I'm talkin about you fuckin me," Toni said with conviction. "I'm sorry I gotta be so blatant but my sister hasn't stopped talking about you, and you only did her one time. It's not just sexual either. You intrigue me to the max Mr. Malik. I thought this was the perfect time to tell you until I saw your woman."

"Toni can we talk about this later," Malik countered. "I hear what you sayin baby, but, I'm with my girl and this is kinda rude."

Toni called Malik's cell phone. It rang. He looked at the screen.

"That's me, lock it in," she said, as she was walking out of the men's room. "No pressure, just call me one time when you're not busy, okay?"

Malik walked out thirty seconds later to see Melissa looking for him by the D.J. booth. She tapped the D.J. and put something in his ear and pointed to Malik. The music stopped abruptly.

"AWWWW," the crowd got restless fast.

"Ladies and gentlemen," said the D.J. "I have a special request from a beautiful lady for a very lucky young man."

A spotlight shined on Malik.

"Today is this guys' birthday. His name is Malik and his girlfriend asked if I could slow it down a bit. She's tryna get her grind on. How could I deny her that? So ya'll gon head and tell my dude Malik happy birthday on the count of the three. 1-2-3," the D.J. pointed his mic at the crowd.

"Happy birthday Malik," mostly women yelled.

"This is Purple Kisses from The Dream's first album. Malik you're a baaaaaad man. Happy birthday broski."

I love the way she put those lips on meeee, purrrple kisses purple kisses on me on me …….

Malik met Melissa in the middle of the dance floor. He caught a glimpse of Toni nearby fanning herself smiling. She mouthed the words, "She's so hot." Malik laughed.

"What's so funny?" asked Melissa.

"Shit, trippin off you baby. That was kinda player. I can't remember if anyone ever pulled something like this before," said Malik. "Nope! Not for me anyway."

"The plan was for you to remember it," Melissa said. "And that's cuz you shoulda been with me."

Melissa kissed him right there on the dance floor. Malik already had his hands on her ass. He squeezed it lightly.

"You ready?" she asked.

"For you," Malik replied.

"That's what I meant."

"One more shot?"

"Whatever you like," said Melissa. "Baby boy you can have whatever you like!"

Other than the red light Malik ran, and the pedestrian he almost hit, he got them home safe. Melissa was drunk and could barely talk straight. As he pulled into the lot Malik scanned the premises before walking into his apartment. He thought he saw someone sitting in a car watching him and Melissa. Once he made it inside the door, he dismissed his paranoid state.

"I gotta piss bad," he said.

Melissa turned out the lights and headed to the bedroom. She took off her jewelry and her belt. She began to unlace the laces from around her calf.

"Nuh uh," uttered Malik. "Leave them on."

Malik walked towards her and kissed her heavily on the lips, reaching underneath her dress, rubbing the warmth of her already wet leopard thong. Malik pushed Melissa onto the foot of the bed quickly pulling down her Victoria's Secret. He inhaled the scent of roses once Melissa was exposed. Pushing up her dress, Malik dove face first into her sex. He French kissed her freshly shaven, overwhelmingly slippery box, licking and slurping every drip of juice he caused her spill. Melissa moaned with delight when Malik spread her folds open and teased her most sensitive area. Melissa squirmed at the pleasure he was giving her.

"Ohhh Malik, baby I love you."

Melissa's comment only made Malik increase the intensity in which he pleased her. He sucked on her impatiently, reaching up inside her dress simultaneously massaging her breast. Flattening his tongue, then folding it up to sop up her juices, he created a flood from her love below.

"Oh my God, please—oh, God don't stop baby," said Melissa, as both hands palmed Malik's head. "Yes—yes—yes … ohhhhhh shit yessss."

Malik continued as Melissa's body jerked and convulsed from her orgasm.

"Baby stop, stop, stop, babbyyyy stop it's too sensitive," she exhaled.

Malik stopped but only to finally take his clothes off. Melissa pulled her dress over her head. He lay on his back, as Melissa eagerly grabbed his erection, put it into her mouthed and rolled her tongue. Malik throbbed against her tongue, wanting more.

"Fuck all that," said Malik. "Sit here."

Melissa sat up and cocked over Malik's body. She slowly guided his thickness between her juicy folds. Melissa stopped at her entrance teasing his head and her lips, rubbing his manhood back and forth against her, then slowly slid down his pole inch by pleasurable inch. Malik grabbed her hips and slowly pulled her all the way down.

"SSSSS," Melissa sucked in her breath.

Palming both ass cheeks, Malik rocked her back and forth until Melissa found a rhythm. Malik stroked her walls, plunging deeper as she descended down his sex.

"Oh you like that," Malik slyly said, already knowing the answer.

"Oh my God I love it baby."

"Get this dick then."

Melissa's eyes were closed, she rolled her hips to the beat of her own song.

"Malik, ohhhh Malik, baby this is your pussy baby. Take this pussy. Get your pussy Daddy."

Malik turned her over on her back in one quick motion.

"Wut you say," Malik dug deeper.

"OOOH, shit this all you—it's yours baby."

Malik put her legs on her shoulders, grabbed her thighs, positioning himself as if he was doing push-ups and plowed deep into the core of her body.

"Oh my God I'm doing—it—a-gainnnn," Melissa exasperated.

"I love this dick," she shouted.

Malik pounded harder, reaching up grabbing her hair, pulling it as he thrust forward.

"You gon cum wit me baby?" she asked.

Malik felt his body twitch.

"Ooooh weee."

His body locked up. He couldn't pull out. He had to surrender to her pleasure. Malik came inside Melissa for the first time. Melissa wrapped her legs around Malik as Malik still laid hard inside her. He grinded slow, and deliberate, showing her he was still ready.

"Damn, baby that's how you feel," asked Melissa. "Ahhh, damn!"

"Yup, that's how I feel."

They never went to sleep.

*

The next few days were ridiculous. Tony, L, Juan, Chuck, and two of Malik's cousins joined him in the stretch charger limousine. They hopped from bar-to-bar, club-to-club, strip club-to-strip club. Eventually, they just did it all in the limo. Making the driver park in front of various clubs showing the owners they rocked harder than the inside. A couple of times they drew the party outside. Women danced in and outside the limo. Malik sprayed Moet in the air every time a female got naked for the squad.

Malik pointed the limo driver towards Detroit without anyone's knowledge. The limo pulled outside of the MGM Grand Casino. Twelve men and women jumped out with bottles of Moet, Remy XO, Grey Goose, and smoking sour diesel. Malik didn't have a reservation, but was lucky they had a suite for the entourage for the night. Everybody was so high and drunk they didn't think about how they would get back to Toledo in the morning. Luckily, Malik's cousin tipped the limo driver. He told him to be back tomorrow by check out time. To top it off Malik won two grand at the roulette table. Chuck won five hundred on black jack. Even Juan, who never gambled won fifteen hundred making side bets. Everyone else quit while they were down. It made for one hell of a weekend.

CHAPTER 8

"Get the fuck back," Roscoe yelled.

He couldn't see their faces, but three men chased him down an alley. He raised his gun, squeezed the trigger. No sound, no blast, no sparks. He checked the clip. It was full. The safety was released. The men kept coming. Roscoe still couldn't make out their faces even though they were only a few feet away from him. He did notice one man's face was distorted. The other two were empty. The men jumped at him, and tackled him to the ground. His vision was stolen. He couldn't move. He couldn't speak. The man with the distorted face, punched a hole through his heart.

"Oh shit," Roscoe woke up breathing heavy sweating profusely. "What da fuck … ."

Roscoe looked around trying to remember where he was. Nothing looked familiar. He looked down and saw the pretty woman with long hair, lying next to him sound asleep. His recollection of the night before was a blur. He had a headache and an unexplainable urge to vomit. Reaching for his keys on the nightstand, Roscoe was turned on by the powder pack lying next to them. Roscoe still hurriedly put on his clothes, stuffed his keys in his pocket, and snatched the pack off the table.

He had been lost for the past few weeks. He blamed his friends' death on himself, and sought to ease his mind by treating his nose. Only he thought he was getting cocaine. Unfortunately for him, it turned out to be the most addicting drug on Earth. She turned out to be lady heroin.

It all started the night of the botched robbery. Roscoe was distraught at losing his friend, and grew more spiteful once he realized he didn't have a dime to show for the loss of three lives. He drove around until he could find a victim. That's when he ran into the pretty woman, with the expensive purse and the seven hundred dollars in it. That night he did find cocaine, and a hotel room for privacy. He'd been getting high ever since.

Roscoe had been on a rampage. In two months he'd robbed three drug dealers, one Check into Cash, four unsuspecting people leaving various bars, Rene, and stole a pair of 24 inch Dub Operas. Altogether, the jack boy accumulated $185,000. Yet, he still lived like a bum. He was on a mission. He stalked his ex-girlfriend every night before he went home, to remind him what his mission was.

A mutual friend turned Roscoe on to where Malik lived. That was the first night his cocaine was replaced with heroin. Roscoe sat in the parking lot waiting for Malik's truck to return. He waited impatiently snorting a couple lines to keep him up. The dealer he got his powder from was the friend of one of those he'd robbed. He mixed the drugs together. As Roscoe waited, he nodded out, coming to just in time to see Malik's truck parked and two figures stumbling into the door.

Now, one month later, Roscoe demanded that same powder, oblivious to what it was. He was upset he blew the chance to surprise Malik, but he worked on a different approach. He was anxious to execute. In due time, he thought.

"Hello," said a scratchy female voice.

"I take it you not up," said Roscoe.

"Who is this," asked the female.

"Oh, this is Jermaine. You gave me your number the other night at the Route. Is this Inez?"

"Yeah, damn Jermaine it's like 8 o'clock in the morning … on a Sunday?"

"Yea my fault," Roscoe said. "I had some other shit going on this morning. I'm thinking everybody should be up if I am. I'll just call you at a better time."

"Okay."

*

Jennifer walked into Chipotle on Secor and Central Avenue to order a burrito bowl for lunch. She was surprised to see the woman she envied in line in front of her. She couldn't help but to notice how beautiful Melissa was in her charcoal gray business suit.

A couple of weeks ago Jennifer followed Melissa for two hours while she ran miscellaneous errands. She followed her to the bank, then the mall, a girlfriends' house, and her mom's house. Eventually, Jennifer began to feel silly. That was her first and last time stalking someone. Today, as she watched Melissa in line she came up with a different plan. If you can't beat em, join em, she thought. She was happy to see Melissa sit down with her order. Jennifer decided to do the same. She sat at a table directly across from Melissa. Jennifer rehearsed her angle.

"Hi," she spoke.

"Hello," Melissa smiled.

"You are so gorgeous," Jennifer said. "I'm sorry to interrupt your meal."

"Oh stop it," Melissa smiled uncontrollably. "Thank you."

"Really," Jennifer started. "I'm sorry I was just eating alone and saw you over there by yourself and I thought, this is terrible when two women, one princess and one maid."

"You must be kidding miss," Melissa said. "You have absolutely the most beautiful tan, and your eyes—you couldn't possibly have trouble dating."

"That's just what I was thinking … do you mind?" Jennifer motioned towards Melissa's table.

"Naw go ahead," said Melissa.

"I was thinking how is it that we're sitting here, alone at lunch time with no male escorts," said Jennifer.

"Sad isn't it," said Melissa.

"Indeed, I bet the only reason your man isn't here is because he's at work making sure you guys are comfortable at home," Jennifer smiled.

"Well, kinda but not really," offered Melissa. "We don't stay together, but he does treat me better than any of the others ever have. I'm not at a complaining stage at the moment."

I'm sure you're not, Jennifer thought.

"Sounds interesting, you looked like one of the lucky ones."

"Actually, it was all luck—the way I met him, purely coincidental," said Melissa.

"I wish," said Jennifer. "I'm an intern at the Toledo Hospital and I'm surrounded by all the supposed smart guys.

Most of them make great money, one third of them are cute, but I just really think I need a change of pace. They bore me a little. I don't want to sound like a hussy, but I'm—I kinda want a black guy."

Melissa laughed. She covered her mouth as it sprung open wide.

"What?" Jennifer asked.

"Nothing you're just—refreshing," said Melissa.

"What does that mean?"

"I like you."

The women finished their meals. Before parting ways, they exchanged numbers. Jennifer smiled all the way back to work. She wondered what had gotten into her. She'd never been conniving before, nor has she ever gone through these lengths for a man.

"Was he really worth it," she thought.

She remembered his touch, and his voice, and the lack of both.

"Absolutely!" she exclaimed.

*

Malik checked his rearview at a red light, more out of habit than paranoia. He noticed a police cruiser behind him in the right lane and an unmarked car, three cars behind them in the left lane. He wasn't dirty but he couldn't help but to wonder if he was about to get pulled over.

Nah, he thought.

The light turned green. He drove off at the same pace as the rest of the traffic, creeping up to the speed limit. He saw an opportunity to turn out of traffic at the store on Hill and Wenz Avenue. After making the turn, Malik parked and got out of the car, only to be approached by a crackhead, asking for change. Malik reached in his cup holder producing a dollar in quarters. As soon as he gave it to the man, squad cars and undercover cars alike surrounded Malik and the crackhead. Malik threw his hands up immediately.

"Get down on the ground," eight officers yelled at once, guns drawn, all aimed at Malik's head.

He followed directions. The detectives ran at him. The first one to get to him was a woman. She dug her knee into his back and yanked at his wrists that were already pressed against each other. Malik knew the routine. The redhead woman detective cuffed him and helped him to his feet.

"Up," she said.

Malik struggled to his feet. He said nothing. Malik watched as the inept officers ransacked his vehicle — tossing C.D.'s around, throwing the contents of the glove box on the floor, Malik smiled.

"What you smilin' at, Hawkins," said Detective Chavez.

Silence.

"Oh you not talkin?"

More silence.

"Don't you wanna know why I'm fuckin with you?" asked Chavez.

"Not particularly, no," Malik answered. "Ya'll dicks, so it's in ya'll nature to be dicks."

"Funny Malik. Listen I am just fucking with you," said Chavez. "But your name came up buddy. Say you got bricks now. Whoa-ho-ho! I always knew you had it in ya. All those times we'd find the little packs you threw. I knew you was working with more than what we lucked up on. Keep it real, last time you went to the joint on that bullshit F-4 you were copping a slab then weren't you?"

"I cut hair for a living Chavez, sorry to disappoint. I've changed my life around."

"That's what I thought until this coward ass nigga got knocked last night—guess what he had Malik?"

Malik shrugged his shoulders.

"A fuckin quarter ounce, and it was his first offense. One thing I can say about you, though. You are one of the few, and trust, I know ya'll by name, who have never snitched. Not once. This is why I believe the chump. Must be somebody important you trying to protect. Am I right?"

"It's called integrity muthafucka."

"Alright, mo money I'm a let you go. But pay attention to the signs Malik. The department couldn't wait until you graduated, or at least heard you did. I know we're a little late," said Chavez. "But you might wanna reconsider piecing out them last couple of thangs. Yea I heard. Bricks! All white bricks!"

Chavez couldn't contain his laugh. The detectives pulled away from the store. Malik collected the c.d. cases and neatly re-stacked them in the back cab. After he put everything else in its proper place, he walked in the store.

"What up homie?" said Ahmed, the corner store clerk.

"I see they are sweating you Malik. You too smart this time, huh?"

"I guess so. Then again maybe not," said Malik, putting a Simply Lemonade on the counter.

A friend of Malik's pulled up in a B.M.W. X5. Malik waited until he got out.

"What's up new money," said Malik.

Malik's friend stepped out, blue button up, blue jeans, blue Yankees fitted, with blue and white Helly Hanson's on his feet.

"I know you aint talkin nigga," said Kevin. "Ole it's my shop I work when I want to ass nigga."

"Yeah I hear you man, I'm just now heading back," said Malik.

"Well shit, let me run in here and follow you back. Can I get first in the chair," asked Kevin.

"Yeah, I got you."

"Aye what was all the police around here for?"

"Me," Malik said plainly.

"Hate to see uh nigga shining don't they."

"Yeah they do, but worse than that, niggas hate to see niggas shining."

"You, aint never lied cuz," said Kevin. "I'll be right back."

Malik jumped in his truck and tried to think who knew about the move. Only Juan and Tony knew, and he knew they weren't telling on him. It had to be some miscellaneous person guessing to save his ass. But why would Chavez say bricks like that, quoting Gucci Mane and Yo Gotti?

Malik contemplated the situation for the 40 minutes it took to cut Kevin's' hair. He knew he shouldn't have gotten greedy, but is fifteen bricks greed, he thought? I mean the squarest nigga could appreciate a gift of fifteen bricks. Suddenly, Dejanique popped in his head. The more he tried to convince himself what he was doing was for their security, the more he realized, he could stop now, use his brain, and would be okay.

Malik concluded that he would stay out of sight, period. Go to work, gym, and back home. He hadn't planned on doing much once the pack came anyway, but now he was certain. He decided he would pay his connect as soon as possible, and turn Juan and Tony on to the plug. He wanted to keep his lil homie under his wing, but wash his hands with the rest of the headaches. The thought was easier than the action. Malik had an incredible urge to see his daughter.

*

Inez called Roscoe two days later. Malik's mother had Dejanique for the night. She decided to see what Jermaine was talking about.

"Hello?" said Jermaine.

"Is this Jermaine?" asked Inez.

"Yeah, who dis?" asked Jermaine.

"*Dis* is Inez. What up early bird?"

Jermaine laughed.

"I guess aint nothing gon stop you from getting that worm."

"Aww naw it aint, but I just had some business to tend to, what's good?"

"Nothing just got off work. Kind of just remembered you called for real," said Inez. "Really I'm off tomorrow I was seeing if your offer was still good."

Roscoe pumped his fist on the other end of the phone. He wondered if he could really finesse the situation. Chances make champions, he thought, so he bit.

"Yea if you aint gon' stand me up. We can get it on."

"Aint nobody getting shit on brotha. I just wanna get to know you and see if we worth each other time," said Inez. "I know a spot on Glendale and Byrne called Doc Watsons?"

"Damn way out there, huh," asked Roscoe.

"Yeah, you wanna meet me there about nine?" asked Inez.

Roscoe wanted to ask why he couldn't pick her up. He decided against it. The same way he decided against telling her his street name.

"Yea that's what's up," he said.

"K, bye."

Inez wanted to ask Malik if he knew Jermaine. She wanted his approval as if Malik were her daddy. Even though Malik's and her relationship seemed to end with their daughter, she began to think Malik wouldn't approve of her seeing anyone period. Inez changed her mind. What's the worst that could happen, she thought. She ran it down in her head—*bad breath, bad sex, no ambition, sheesh.*

"Fuck it," Inez said out loud as she turned on the shower. "Can't be any worse than the rest."

So she thought.

*

Toni was at work observing a heart surgery although her field of study was anesthesiology. Toni watched intensely as the surgeon closed off one artery, using his left hand to elevate the heart, while another doctor squeezed water from a bottle to flush the blood away from the heart.

After a while Toni went into a trance. She thought about the heart and how fragile it really is. The veins, arteries, and ventricles were all strings helping the heart pump life into the body. The same way emotions tug on it and make people do the strange things they do, because of love, or the need for it. She wondered how she could be so driven to lure someone into her heart that was already in the heart of someone else. It seemed wrong and deceitful, even though she didn't know Melissa, she knew she would befriend her in a minute if Malik chose her. Right on cue her phone rang.

"What's up Toni?" said Malik.

Toni looked at her phone, at the name, and smiled.

"Malik?"

"Toni?"

"Oh shut up it's not like you call every day."

"And it's not every day beautiful women follow me to the bathroom"

"Touché', what's good pimpin," said Toni.

Malik busted into laughter.

"Shit you tell me. You the one was so aggressive the other night," Malik said. "I figured you had a lot on your mind. But then again, you aint got that courage juice in you now, so I guess you tongue tied now."

"Not exactly," said Toni. "I was just thinking about—a situation here at work."

"I don't mean to cut you off but where do you and your sister work," he asked. "Cuz ya'll holdin'."

"Ha, hardly. She's began to make some money," Toni said. "She's a radiologist, and I'm studying to become an anesthesiologist."

"Damn," said Malik. "Well can't say ya'll aint gotcha mind right. My fault I cut you off. Good luck with that though. I hope it work out for you."

"Yeah, thanks. See that's that shit right there."

"What," said Malik confused.

"How your so—I don't know … Do you know what I think is the sexiest thing about a man?"

"Nope, but I'm sure you gon' tell me."

"His ability to be himself and his mystique," she said. "It's like you carry this confidence about you. You swag different than the rest, at least in my opinion you do. You're cute, you have a nice body, you take care of your business. Somehow it seems to me you make women feel as if they lose out by not choosing you. It's borderline arrogance, yet you never say why they miss out, so it's not quite arrogance. Then you're all hood, but then you turn it off whenever—ahhhh— you're driving me crazy."

"So, what you're saying is," asked Malik.

Toni's lips pouted as she pondered the question.

"I'm sayin you're a sexy motherfucker, and I wanna do something to you. At first I was going be stingy, but I had an epiphany of sorts so, I want to respect the fact that I can't have you to myself, but I know—can I please just get some of your time? Fuck it. I just like you. I just wanna be around you—a friend to you—anything you want me to be."

Malik smiled a big huge smile. He couldn't control it. He was used to women being perplexed about his persona. Once they got to know him, conversations like the one he was having were quite common. For one reason or another he respected Toni. Malik didn't always play so hard to get. Melissa had affected him big time. A couple years prior, Malik would've accepted the situation for what it was. He was different somehow, changing for the better, so he thought.

"I can respect that, but what about your sister," asked Malik. "What about L?"

"I've thought about that. Basically, my sister feels the same way I do. We've discussed you, and she's cool with it. As a matter of fact you'll be overwhelmed here shortly," Toni laughed. "L on the other hand—We mesh well if I could party all the time. I can't, and we both know he's a for the moment type of guy."

"I get all that but did you tell him you was feelin me too?"

"Yeah, I did. His feelings weren't hurt. He asked me what's up my sister," Toni chuckled.

"That's my dogg," Malik chimed in.

"Well I'm glad I got that off my chest," said Toni.

"Yeah, me too. No more scaring the piss outta me in the boys bathroom, right?"

"Nope."

"Good," said Malik. "I gotta go. We'll holler later."

"Bye."

*

"How you get this number dude?" asked Melissa.

"I just wanted to tal … ."

"There isn't anything to talk JJ," she said. "I'm not on you. I don't want talk to you."

"Mel I just wanna holla atchu," JJ pleaded. "Why you keep playin me like this? I miss you baby. I'm sorry bout the past. You fuckin wit dat lame like he aint never go to jail or nothing. What you gon do when he get locked up. He prolly can't even fill my shoes."

Melissa sat for a moment. Truthfully, it was a good question. Malik didn't hustle anymore, she thought. Either way, she wasn't about to let JJ know that she was worried. She knew Malik was up to something, but she also knew he wasn't consumed by that something.

"JJ, you'll never be half the man Malik used to be. I was a kid when we were together. You were like twenty-six when I was seventeen. I didn't tell you to go rob anybody," she explained. "I told you I liked you regardless if you had money or not. There's no way you could've expected me—what was I eighteen when you left — an eighteen year old young lady to wait patiently for a supposedly grown man that didn't have his shit together. Malik is my sun and I am his earth. You're calling me spitting venom, hating and everything. Trust me baby you are not even in his league."

"Fuck you den bitch," JJ screamed. "That nigga sell dope like everybody else, and you know you aint the only one he fuckin you."

Click.

"Hello," JJ said. "Hello."

Melissa couldn't listen to the pointless conversation anymore. She recalled the time when she met JJ. He was older, and kind of charming. He seemed like someone with goals and direction. Melissa's young mind couldn't see that he was gaming her from the jump.

JJ noticed how her beauty affected all men. He couldn't handle it. He accused her of cheating. He slapped her around a few times for not calling when she got home from a party or with her friends. Finally, JJ became obsessed with her. He convinced himself if he had enough money to where she didn't have to work or lift a finger, she would be his forever. Eight years later, the realization of that false sense of security burned through his soul as if it were trapped in the basement of hell. He was determined to get Melissa back, one way or the other.

Melissa was furious. She needed somebody to talk to. She tried her friend Jessica. But Jessica had been so consumed in her studies and with her relationship that they hadn't talked much. The last time she and Jessica really spent time together was the day she met Malik. That was months ago. The more Melissa thought about Jessica, the more worried she became. Even though they had a light conversation here and there something was odd. It was unlike Jessica not to show her face. Melissa decided to call her friend again.

The phone rang and rang until her voicemail picked up.

"Jessi, this is Mel, just wondering if you were okay. Damn I aint your girl no more? Call me immediately, bye."

Jessica's face popped into Melissa's mind. She pictured her yellow skin, dark brown eyes that seemed to be black. She had jet-black hair that she usually kept in tight, spiral curls, and a cute thin nose that tapered into the thickest, prettiest lips. She wondered were her girlfriend could be. Melissa began to worry more, and the more she worried, the more Jessica's smile carved itself into Melissa's thoughts.

Melissa let it go for now. She still wanted to talk to somebody, other than Malik about JJ's ignorant ass. She had a thought but dismissed it quickly. Then Melissa thought about her again, an impartial person, oblivious to the past and the present. Should she call Jennifer? *I just met her*, thought Melissa. Jennifer seemed cool, down to earth enough to understand. What the hell, why not?

"Who dis?" asked Jennifer.

She made her voice deep like a man's. If she would've looked at the caller i.d. she would've known.

"Umm Melissa."

"Oh hey," said Jennifer. "Sorry I was just being silly, and bored to death. How are you?"

"Ha! Funny you asked. I called cuz I needed somebody to talk to. I wouldn't have bothered you but ... ."

"It's okay honey what's wrong," said Jennifer sounding genuinely concerned.

"Well ... you wanna meet me for a drink?"

"Oh that bad, huh? Sure, where?"

"Do you know where Arnie's is?" asked Melissa.

"Ummm ... I think so," Jennifer answered. "On Central and Secor?"

"Yup, I'll be there in a half an hour."

"K, me too."

Exactly fifty minutes from the time the two women hung up, they were ordering margaritas, sitting across from one another in a booth at Arnie's. Jennifer wore a white belly shirt, with blue writing on it that read, *eat me if you're hungry.* Her low-rise jeans clung to her body like a wet napkin. Her blonde hair had dark brown streaks flowing through the waviness.

Jennifer stared Melissa in the eyes. This woman is flawless, thought Jennifer. Melissa had on no make-up. She sat there, au natural, wearing a long jean skirt and a short sleeve button up shirt, looking distraught, somehow making more gorgeous.

"Here you go ladies. Two mango margaritas," said Sharon, their waitress. "Just wave when you're ready."

"Thank you," said Jennifer.

"Oh by the way, your shirt is great," said Sharon.

Jennifer poked out her chest as if reading it for the first time. She smiled.

"You like?"

"Indeed," Sharon held her gaze just long enough to let Jennifer know just how much she liked it.

Sharon walked off cheesing.

"That shirt is definitely a conversation starter," said Melissa as she sipped the margarita.

"Mmm, so listen," she continued. "I got a call from an old boyfriend today."

"Oh gotcha thinkin about him?" Jennifer countered. "Or complete asshole, like all the others?"

"Complete asshole like all the others," said Melissa. "He calls me trying to get me back, but he's hating the whole time, telling me Malik does this, Malik does that."

"Who's Malik?"

"Oh, right. Malik is my kindred spirit. He's like my best friend and all that. Wouldn't know what I'd do without him," Melissa said. "If he doesn't ask me to marry him within the next year, I'll probably ask him myself."

"Ooookay! Malik's an African King, yes?"

"Indeed," said Melissa.

She proceeded to tell her story. At the end Jennifer realized she wouldn't have had much ammunition to persecute Melissa anyway. Furthermore, she started to feel more and more like a friend to Melissa, especially after their third margarita.

By now they both were talking. Jennifer spoke about old boyfriends. She even had a slip of the tongue about a girl, girl situation. Jennifer was convinced Melissa was a good person when she responded.

"Who am I to judge, but I don't think, as far as ego is concerned that two women could co-exist in a union between one another," Melissa continued. "But was it fun?"

Jennifer smiled from ear to ear, and blushed through her tan. She shook her head.

"Aaaab-so-lutely," Jennifer's head dropped as she chuckled. "Don't get me wrong, dick still rules the nation, but the sensuality of a woman kissing, hugging, rubbing, and touching, you is just a whole other experience."

Melissa felt her face get warm as she smiled and blushed as she thought about what Jennifer was saying. Truthfully, she hadn't ever given it a thought. Looking at Jennifer's pretty face and phenomenal body, Melissa admitted to herself she hadn't ruled it out either.

"Girl you are wild," said Melissa.

"Am I?"

"Indeed you are," Melissa said. "Let's karaoke."

They jumped up, hand in hand, grabbed the microphone and performed Prince's Purple Rain. The whole bar offered their assistance. Before long the entire bar, sang together.

"Purple rain! Purple rain!"

Melissa and Jennifer walked off the mock stage. The whole bar cheered, and whistled. Sharon, their waitress, poured them each a double shot of tequila, on the house. Each woman threw her shot back quick, and with ease. The Cuervo twisted their faces a little, but it was a party.

The night was getting long. They arrived at six o'clock and already it was ten-thirty. Jennifer grabbed Melissa's hand.

"Let's go," said Jennifer.

The women stumbled out of the bar, into the parking lot. They laughed under the night sky into the warm air.

"Oh, I feel so much better," said Melissa. "You are the best Ms. Jennifer, had a great time."

"Glad I could help. What are you about to do now?"

"Call Malik, for a little night cap."

"You're so bad."

Melissa leaned in to hug Jennifer. Jennifer knew it was meant to be a hug, but she kissed Melissa anyway. Melissa was shocked, almost paralyzed at the touch of Jennifer's lips. However, she let Jennifer kiss her. Her lips were soft and pleasing. Jennifer pulled away, lightly licking Melissa's top lip.

"Yeah, a lil drunk here," said Melissa. "I gotta go."

Jennifer put her head down and smiled.

"Sorry, you're just so fun and beautiful. Your lip-gloss is poppin, what can I say," said a laughing Jennifer.

"No worries. I thought you probably might anyway. But on that note, I gotta go."

"Bye."

"Bye."

Melissa jumped in her Monte Carlo calling Malik immediately.

"Hello?" answered Malik.

"Babe, where you at?"

"Home," he said. "Why, what's up? You cool? You sound lit."

"I'm fine. Yes I have been drinking, and I need your services."

"Is that right?"

"Yesssir. Is there a problem," asked Melissa.

"Not at all."

"Well I'm on my way."

"What's taking you so long then?"

*

The next day after Melissa got off work, she tried to call Jessica. Ring. Ring. But still, there was no answer.

Melissa decided to go over to her house. As she pulled up to the house on Gretna Green, Melissa noticed Jessica's black Grand Cherokee sitting at the curb in front of the house. Melissa thought it was odd because Jessica usually parked in the garage, or in the driveway. Melissa walked to the front door, unconscious glancing inside the truck. The passenger door was shut, but the dome light was on. She went to the driver's side door and shut it tightly.

Something wasn't right. Melissa felt her blood go cold. She ran to the door, knocked.

"Oh my God," said Melissa.

The door flew open. Jessica's boyfriend was rushing out of the house. He looked disoriented, and shocked.

"Melissa?" Tony asked with a fake smile on his face. "Where you come from?"

"I came to check on Jessi. I haven't seen her in so long," Melissa said as she tried to nonchalantly, push past the door. "Is she here?"

"No."

"Where is she?"

"I don't know," Tony replied. "She said she had some studying to do."

"Well, why is her car here?" Melissa countered.

"My piece of shit broke down on me," Tony replied. "She let me whip her shit around. Somebody came and got her this afternoon to go to class."

Melissa stared at Troy's barreled chest, slight gut, and massive arms. He stood six feet even, but he was a big man. His chocolate face was blank. His lips were twisted upward, causing the goatee he wore to slant. Troy's brown eyes were screaming with rage and Troy had a brand new Audi, far from a piece of shit. Melissa knew better than to ask questions.

"Well tell her yellow ass to call me when she get back," she cautiously said. "I need to holler at her."

Troy changed his demeanor.

"Yup, soon as she get here Melly Mel."

"Bye."

Melissa walked to her car. She drove around the corner, circled the block a couple of times until the Cherokee was gone. She pulled back up to her friends' residence, ran to the door and banged hard.

"Jessi. Jessi. Jessi," Melissa yelled.

No answer.

She ran to the window to peek in. She couldn't see a thing. The curtains were drawn shut. Melissa ran around to the back door. She banged again, tapping on the kitchen window still yelling Jessi's name. Still, there was no answer. Melissa stood there frustrated. She sat on the back porch, thinking unpleasant things. A single tear raced down her face.

*

Jessica lay on the floor of her bedroom helpless. Her naked body was bruised all over. Her once radiant, yellow skin, was now blemished with the ugliest of greens, the deepest purples, and darkest blacks. She tried to move, but couldn't. A broken rib made it unbearable to even crawl. It even hurt her to breathe. Jessica heard the banging on the door, but it stopped. It restarted about ten minutes later, after Troy came back and told her she'd *better shut the fuck up.* Who could it be, she thought. Then it hit her like lightening. Melissa, Jessica thought. She knew Melissa would never give up on her if she thought something was wrong.

Troy began beating her a few months ago when she became pregnant. She hadn't had much contact with Melissa since. Now her life depended on her simply making a noise. The second series of banging stopped. Jessica wanted to cry. She couldn't. She needed to survive.

Jessica was upstairs. She needed to get down the stairs to Melissa. She looked up at the bedroom window. All she had to do was crawl ten feet to get there, and raise up to be seen. Her rib was cracked on her left side. It took every ounce of strength that she had in her one hundred thirty-two pound body to turn over on her right side. Jessica gripped the carpet with her right elbow and forearm and pushed forward with her right foot. The task was excruciating. She grimaced with every movement — propping up on her nightstand — she caught her breath.

The window was two feet in front of her. Jessi knew she couldn't lift the window, but she was sure if she stood there, Melissa, or whoever could and would see her. Jessica gathered herself, using the weight of her right side only. She triumphantly stood up at the window just in time to see Melissa's white Monte Carlo pulling onto Dorr Street. She couldn't control her sobbing this time.

CHAPTER 9

"What's up boi?" said Malik over the music.

I am a Roc representa, summer to winter dead or alive, one c.d. or 360 pies.

Charmaine turned the Jay-z down walking towards the back room. Juan walked in wearing a black and gold Crown Holder t-shirt and matching jeans, Creative Recreations on his feet.

"What it do cuzin?" said Juan.

He lifted stacks of money from around his waist. He threw it all in Malik's' lap.

"Boy you put that shit together?"

"A lil bit at first, till Chavez bitch ass jumped out on me why?" Malik said. "its dat leap frog, aint it."

"Man. Damn, its been a long time since I've seen some shit like that," Juan said.

"Cut it out nigga. This was some lucky shit that happened. Let me stress the word *lucky.* We both know the truth."

"Whatever you that dude right now mufucka, let me say that," said Juan. "I'm really feelin you right now—pause."

Both Juan and Malik busted out in laughter.

"What's this?" asked Malik.

"Sixty of the damndest," said Juan.

"That's why I fucks wit you my nigga," Malik said. "You know you don't play no games."

"Aw man, look here I got kids and shit. They got playtime I don't, feel me?"

"Well look here bro," Malik countered. "I'm thinkin it's time to make bigger and better moves."

"Like what? I'm always lookin foe some legit shit to do."

"Man I'm just not feelin this shit no more. Mufuckas telling on me and don't even know me bro," said Malik. "It's time for me to step aside if only for a little bit, you feel me? I'm tryna to get into anything that's profitable, so you know just think on it. Anyway, I got six left."

"Damn you a beast, from Christine?" Juan said. "Whew! Must be nice."

Malik smiled hard, laughing wholeheartedly. It was nice. He deserved to be on his shit. He couldn't see it know other way.

"Yeah, but without you I aint shit cumin," Malik said.

"I hear you mufucka," said Juan. "This shit here, sell itself all day."

"I bought you a couple fits from New York Collection," Malik said. "It's about three fits over there."

Malik nodded towards the gray and blue bags from the store. Juan walked over, picked up the bags.

"Hmmmm, heavy," said Juan.

"You know dat. But uhhh. Take your time my nigga I got fam squared away. I told him what I was thinking. He couldn't blame me. So, I put a word in for you. He going to be one hunned just as long as you one hunned, feel me?

"Damn you serious as hell huh?" asked Juan.

"Man I can't—" Malik said. "I'm winning. I gotta gracefully bow out. How many mufuckas you know get outta this shit on they own terms? Riddle me that."

"Feel you," Juan said. "I got you my nigga. I'm out cheah. Be my eyes."

"Got you."

Malik was quiet on the other end of the phone until Juan was outside.

"You good doggy," Malik said. "Let me know you made it," said Malik.

"Alright, good lookin."

Juan pulled away in a black Lincoln MK7 rental car. Malik saw everything was good and sat down. Charmaine walked back into the living room. Malik looked her up and down.

"What you lookin at dude?" asked Malik.

"I'm proud of you," said Charmaine.

"Why?"

"Cuz I overheard what you told Juan."

"You mean you were ear hustling," Malik cut her off.

"Shut up. So, are you for real?" she asked. "Are you done? I knew you were smarter than that. I just ... I always have known you to hustle. It's gon' be weird."

"How is it gon be weird for you?"

"No more extra money. No outrageous requests," said Charmaine. "No more worrying about you at night, wondering if you are alright."

Charmaine looked at the floor, playing with her hands. Malik stared at her in her Seven jeans. She wore them well. Malik heard her loud and clear. He wished he hadn't. The mixed emotions he had about Charmaine conflicted with everything.

Malik thought back to that night at the Shadow Lounge when he met Charmaine. He was playing it cool because he saw all the other niggas in the spot losing theirs. She walked past the bar and sat down on a green couch with a girlfriend. Malik noticed the closeness between them as he continued to pretend he wasn't paying them any attention. Her friend swayed to the bar and ordered a drink right next to him.

"Can I get two blue mufuckas please?"

Malik didn't try to hide his staring this time because the girl was an astonishing Puerto Rican. Her hair was cut just past her shoulders. She rocked a navy blue Dona Karan skirt with a white belt and some white Jimmy Choos. The body on this lady was too much for his eyes to compute. However, being the player that he considered himself to be, Malik turned away from her and ordered a drink of his own.

"Let me get a double of Ciroc, and two blue mufuckas, and can you get em to those two ladies over there."

Malik watched as the waitress took the two drinks over to the ladies. They smiled when she pointed to Malik posing at the bar. He raised his glass, and they motioned him to them. He obliged.

"What we gonna do with these?" asked Charmaine. "You know you just saw her order these ones. You think you slick."

"Damn, my bad I was just contributing to the party," Malik said. "Ya'll deserve it, ya'll winning tonight. I thought I should congratulate ya'll."

"Well since you put it that way, thank you sir. My name is Maria and this is my intoxicated friend Charmaine."

"How ya'll doing? I'm Malik," Malik said as he tried his hardest to keep his composure.

The two women looked totally out of place. To say they were winning was an absolute understatement. If they were winning it was like the 96' Bulls. The Shadow was rocking nonetheless. Young Jeezy came through the speakers as everybody sang 'bitch I'm amazin look what I'm blazin eyes so low man I look like an Asian.' Malik extended his hand as the trio met for the first time.

"I aint want shit I was just feelin the fuck outta ya'll swag," said Malik. "I don't wanna intrude on ya'll little party, just get with me before ya'll leave."

"Aw nigga don't play that role. We feelin' you," said Maria. "You mean to tell me your cool ass ran outta steam that fast?"

They all started laughing.

"That's funny, but naw baby, I aint run out of steam I was just giving you your space, if you ready for a sample I'm ready to give you a taste, feel me," said Malik.

They all laughed like they were at the Comedy Connection.

"I knew you had it in you," said Charmaine.

Maria shot her a funny look.

Charmaine returned the scowl.

"Well let's see what you talkin about daddy," said Maria.

The rest was history. The two ladies escorted Malik out of the club and followed him to a strip club. He gave them ones to throw at the women. From there they went to White Tower, an all-night diner that served the night owls of the city some of the best butter burgers in Toledo.

Maria and Malik were on each other tough after that. The next six months was party and bullshit for Malik, Maria, and Charmaine. Charmaine remained in the mix because she had no man. Most of the men she encountered were either imposters or too submissive to her. Deep down she wished Malik would've chose her, but Maria was more aggressive while, Charmaine didn't stake her claim, so naturally Malik went for the woman that showed the most interest. In the meantime Malik didn't mind Charmaine tagging along. He often asked her to join. They went to concerts, Bilal Park in Detroit, the Jazz Festival in Cincinnati. They had fun together.

One night Maria and Charmaine had a ladies night out, while Malik let his phone lead him around the city. The ladies were surprisingly sober that night on their way home leaving Vamps. The night was a total lost. Maria decided to call Malik, just as she pressed the send button he was calling.

"Hello?" said Malik.

"Yea," said Maria. "I was just calling you."

"Oh, fa real? What's up what you doin? You fuckin wit me?"

"Damn can I answer nigga."

"Long as you answer right."

"Well, if you want me to," Maria said. "I gotta drop Charmaine off though."

"That's cool," Malik said. "Shiiiit she can sleep on the couch if you don't feel like it. You know that's my nigga."

"Naw," she said. "I don't want her to hear us fuckin."

"So, it aint like she haven't before."

"You so nasty."

"That's why you love me."

"I don't know why I love your retarded ass, but I do."

Malik didn't respond. Maria never admitted that she loved him before. He wanted to retreat, but didn't know why.

"So ya'll on the way?" he asked.

"Yea I guess nasty ass."

The phone went dead.

Malik snapped out of his thoughts.

"Girl I aint going nowhere. I'm just done trappin," said Malik. "You still my ne-ge-ro."

Charmaine collapsed onto Malik's lap.

"Listen here little fucker," said Charmaine. "I know Melly Mel is your chick, but if you ever walk out of my life I'm a kill you – and that bitch."

Charmaine gave Malik a peck on the lips and got up.

"Damn you shrewd, but I'm fa damn sho keep that in mind doggy, you ready?"

"Yup."

Charmaine grabbed the drugs, and Malik grabbed the money. Charmaine followed Malik to a house she'd never seen before. He went in and came out in five minutes later. She followed him again to drop off the money at a house she'd seen often.

Malik's cousins' house was nice. It was white brick, with gated doors, picture windows, basketball rim, swimming pool, and a horseshoe driveway. Inside, the home was just as immaculate. Again, Malik went in for five minutes and walked back out. He made Charmaine drive his truck, and leave her car behind.

"Where we headed captain?" asked Charmaine.

"You hungry?"

"Yes sir."

"Bennihana it is."

"Malik its seven twenty," said Charmaine. "We gon make it? What time they close?"

"We going to make it long as you drive this muthafucka."

*

It had been hours since Troy left Jessica on the floor passed out. He'd taken her cell phone. There wasn't a house phone to use. Ever since Jessica saw Melissa pull off, she lost hope sitting on the table next to the window, in pain, naked, bruised, with dried blood on her swollen face. Jessica was close to going into shock. She was sure if Troy came back before anyone found out what was going on, he'd kill her.

Suddenly, there was the sound of a horn outside. Again, Jessica struggled to pull herself up to the window. She stared intently through the window at the darkening sky. There were no lights on in the house. Jessica focused on the car in her driveway. It was her faithful friend Melissa again. She must've sensed something was wrong, thought Jessica. Jessica had an idea.

Melissa honked her horn frantically at the house, hoping the sound would summon her friend out of whatever unconscious state she was in. In between the time Melissa left, she went to Jessica's mother's home. Neither her mother nor her sister had seen her or spoken to her in over two weeks. Melissa was convinced something was wrong. She dialed Jessica's phone again, and again no answer.

Honk! Honk! Honk!

Melissa held the horn for a long time. After she rubbed the tears from her eyes, she thought she was tripping. The lights from Jessi's bedroom began to flicker. Jessica was in there, but why wouldn't she just open the door. Something must be wrong, thought Melissa. Melissa ran to the neighbor house, pounded on the door.

"Yes?"

A confused middle aged black woman, wearing a pair of plastic, wide rimmed reading glasses answered the door.

"Hi, um, I'm Melissa—a friend of your neighbor— I ... this might sound crazy but I think my friend is hurt really bad and can't come to the door. Can you help me please?" begged Melissa.

The woman noticed the panic on the young lady's face. Something was definitely wrong.

"What do you think is wrong?" asked the lady.

"She's my best friend and I haven't seen her in weeks, and now she's not answering the phone, or the door, but the lights are flickering on and off—I know she's—can you please just help?" Melissa pleaded and sobbed.

"John, you might want to come here a minute honey," yelled the woman.

The woman explained everything to her husband John. He went outside to find anything out of the ordinary and sure enough the lights were still flickering from inside.

"Well I don't know what's wrong, but something aint right," explained John. "If she don't answer the door, I'm gonna break it down."

After a few knocks, and no response, John gripped the hammer he'd brought, and dismantled the top lock. He ran upstairs into the bathroom, witnessing his once gorgeous neighbor looking as if she just went a couple rounds with Mike Tyson in his prime.

"Jessica," he called out to her.

She stood there unresponsive, still flicking the light switch. John grabbed a blanket off the bed, wrapped her naked body, and carried her down the stairs. As he walked with her outside he noticed the Cherokee that usually sat in the driveway speed past. John carried Jessica to his house. He laid her on the couch.

"Call the police Ann."

Melissa stared in disbelief. She couldn't even tell if it was Jessica or not. Jessica was so severely beaten that her eyes were slits. No one could tell if they were opened or closed.

"Jessi, I'm sooo sorry babe. I didn't mean to leave you here earlier—I didn't know," said Melissa.

"Yeah, I just saw that boyfriend of hers speeding down the street like he lost his damn mind," John said. "Fucker looked right at me. I bet he did all of this."

"I'm fucking him up," said Melissa. "I'm gonna kill 'em."

"Now relax young lady. That coward probably would be terrified of you. He's a pussy. You say you were here earlier?" asked John. What happened?"

Melissa broke down as she recalled the events of the day.

"Well we going tell the police just that," said John.

Ann tried to give Jessica some tea. It rolled out the corner of her mouth. The police pulled up with an ambulance and the Fire Department.

John told his story to the police. Melissa followed the ambulance to the Medical College of Ohio, where she gave her statement to police. Afterwards, she'd learned Jessica had a sprained ankle, a broken jaw, a cracked rib, deep tissue bruising, and some internal bleeding. She was being monitored closely in the I.C.U. where she laid in a coma.

"She's lucky to be alive miss," said Dr. Wassan. "Had you not taken action when you did she would've been dead within the next couple of hours or so. With that said, she's still not completely out of the woods. There are a ton of things that can still go wrong."

Melissa didn't know whether to be relieved or to cry again.

"Can I stay with her?" asked Melissa.

"Well ... I'll allow it for the night, don't try to wake her or disturb her she's very fragile right now," the doctor said. "I urge you to call her mother or sister. This is still a sensitive issue. But you did a great thing ma'am. I wish all my patients had a friend like you."

Melissa forced a smile.

"Thanks."

Melissa called Jessica's mother and sister. They were there in ten minutes and stayed at least twenty minutes away. Once in the room they said a prayer for Jessica. Melissa walked out to call Malik, and told him the news.

"What?" Malik asked in disbelief. "You bullshittin. Damn that's fucked up. You want me to come?"

"Naw, her mom and sister are here. I called to tell you I'm probably gonna be here for the night," Melissa's voice broke.

"Baby I'm sorry. But she going to be alright. You're an angel. You saved her baby. You need anything? You want me to do anything?"

Melissa thought about the question. She wanted Troy dead. Jail wasn't enough. She'd never seen anyone beaten so badly.

"No, I'm fine."

"Well call me and let me know what's up."

"I love you so much," said Melissa.

"Love you too."

CHAPTER 10

Inez walked up to the door of her house, Dejanique in one hand, fumbling with her keys with the other. She put Dejanique down to unlock the door. As soon as Inez got the door open, somebody ran from the side of her house, covered her mouth with a huge hand, picking her up with ease. Another masked man picked up the baby, closed the door to Inez's home, and calmly walked to the van parked across the street.

"That was easier than I thought," said one kidnapper.

"Let me go muthafucka, dumb bitch's, my baby daddy gon kill you niggaz."

"Shut up bitch."

Something about the voice startled Inez

"Fuck you bitch ass nigga!"

Whap! A hand came out of nowhere, knocking Inez out cold. Dejanique began to cry. One kidnapper put her pacifier in her mouth. Dejanique spat it out.

"Man I can't deal with no cryin' babies," the other kidnapper said.

"Well you going to have to deal with it, that's our bread and butter right there," the other one said. "Shhh Deja, Dejaaa. What's the matter baby? I'm not gonna hurt you yet."

*

"Hook me up some links with them grits, I'm hungry than a muthafucka," yelled Tony.

Malik was in the kitchen making omelets with turkey bacon, and deli sliced turkey breast.

"Nigga Rachel Ray couldn't do this shit better. Nigga you think my name is Chauncey?" said Malik. "It's too early foe that bullshit."

"Dude it's eleven o'clock."

Malik walked out of his kitchen with an omelet and hash browns.

"Get your own juice," said Malik already taking care of his meal.

"Damn, like dat?" Tony asked.

"Nigga, I aint yo bitch," said Malik. "Ungrateful ass nigga—gimme my omelet back."

Tony snatched his plate out of the reach of Malik.

"Damn, alright brotha. I'm a get my own."

The two men ate, and played a quick game of 2K10. Afterwards, they decided to go to Best Buy. Tony remembered he needed to take his laptop to the Geek Squad.

"You know a nigga named JJ?" asked Tony.

"Naw, what about him?"

"I guess he used to fuck wit Melissa. Boy you must got a mean stroke, no homo, but I guess he salty at you about her," said Tony.

"J.J. huh?" Malik pondered. "Ain't the nigga Roscoe real name Jermaine?"

"Yeah, Jermaine Johnston," Tony replied. "Never really thought about that fa real."

"So you mean to tell me all this time I been thinkin Roscoe was the one—damn who is his bitch?"

"I don't know, but he still a problem cuz he been out here wildin," said Tony.

"Man let me call baby to get to the bottom of this shit," Malik said. "Now that I think about it, I never did ask her who dude was I just assumed it was what you wuz telling me about before. Hold on."

"He-ll-o?"

"Baby what's wrong?"

"Ma-a-a-lik … she's gone. She gone baby. Jessi's gone."

Melissa began to let it all out, as if saying those words out loud brought her to realization of the truth.

"Aw naw," said Malik. "Damn that's fucked up."

"What's wrong?" Tony asked.

"You know," Malik raised his finger signaling Tony to hold on.

"Babe I'm bout to come up there."

"O-o-kay," she sniffled. "I'm at M.C.O. babe."

"Me and Tony on the way."

Malik told Tony what was going on. Tony genuinely felt bad for Jessica. She was a good girl even though he didn't know her that well. Malik told Tony about the night before, about her soft ass boyfriend, and how they found her. Both Tony and Malik began to get irate. Twenty minutes later Tony pulled up to the main entrance of M.C.O. Malik went inside alone. His phone rang.

"Inez," said Malik to himself as he looked at his phone.

"I can't talk right now," Malik pressed the end button and held it.

Malik took the elevator to the third floor I.C.U. No sooner than the doors opened, Malik witnessed his girlfriend, sitting in the lobby, paralyzed with pain. Malik has dealt with death on many different levels throughout his life. He often questioned his emotional state due to the fact that it was hard for him to grieve. If one lives he has to die. Malik didn't welcome death, but it was hard for him to walk through life without admitting that fact.

Melissa sat in silence. She hadn't even noticed Malik sitting next to her. Her eyes were distant, carrying bags of grief beneath them. Her lips were dry, hair uncombed, face chiseled in disbelief. Malik got on his knees in front of her, clutching her hands. Melissa's tears began to flow again.

"Baby let me get you outta here," said Malik.

"You're only making yourself hurt worse," he continued. "Let me take you home babe."

Melissa hugged Malik tight. She didn't let go for a full two minutes. Finally, Malik rose to his feet, grabbed her by the hand, wrapped his arms around her waist from behind. They walked to the elevator as one.

*

Inez woke up in bed. She thought she was at home until she felt the handcuffs slicing through her wrists. Her eyes opened, no one occupied the filthy room with her. The windows were boarded, there was junk of all kinds laying everywhere on the floor. Inez looked at the door, ran to it. She pulled it, shook it, kicked it, nothing happened. Her chest constricted. She could hardly breathe, looking around frantically.

"Deja," Inez yelled. "Deja! Gimme my baby please— Deja!"

Inez continued to yell until her throat hurt. Finally, a shadow formed underneath the door. Inez didn't stop screaming.

"Just gimme my daughter," she cried.

"Aye, man, shut-the-fuck-up," one of the masked men walked through the door. "Your daughter is cool. Why would I leave her with you while you were knocked out. That's stupid Inez."

"Why are you doing this?" she pleaded. "This is stupid."

"Not really," the masked man said. "I'm really not feeling your dude."

"He aint my dude," she replied. "We're not even together."

"I know that. Let me ask you a ... ."

"Wait—where the other nigga at from last night?"

"Don't worry about him."

"Where is my daughter?"

"Downstairs."

"Bring her to me please."

Inez didn't care about anything, but her daughter at the moment. She didn't care if they killed her, raped her, or tortured her, as long as Dejanique was fine she would welcome death. What she didn't know, was the strangers were taking good care of Dejanique. Most people couldn't imagine a kidnapper doing well by their child. However, the truth was the truth.

"Alright," the kidnapper walked to the door, yelling for the baby and sat down next to Inez on the twin-sized bed.

"How much is your baby daddy worth?"

"What?"

"You heard me."

"I don't know," she replied. "What you holding us for ransom or something?"

"I guess so," he countered. "So, estimate for me."

"Dude, I really don't know. He doesn't buy me shit anymore. He don't confide in me about his savings. He takes care of his daughter. Whatever she needs he gets," she said. "How you aint do your homework before committing to something like this?"

"I know up and about," he said. "I just don't know what I can realistically get out of him."

"Just please call and ask him. He'll pay, I'm sure. Just please don't be dumb and ask for nothing crazy."

Something crazy was what he wanted. Truthfully, she was right. In order for the kidnapping to be successful, the amount of money should be easily accessible. Fifty thousand, one hundred the kidnapper thought.

"Fuck it I'll settle for a hundred grand after me and my dude split it fifty cool," he said. "What you think?"

"I don't know I told you where my."

The door cracked open. Then Inez heard someone race back downstairs. She practically ran to the door. Dejanique was smiling in her car seat. She didn't stink either, which meant these guys actually changed her diaper, or at least had someone do it.

"I told you she was alright," said the kidnapper. "So listen, do this nigga got another number or what cuz he aint answerin. To tell the truth he cut the phone off after the first time I called. He must hate yo guts."

"Ha! Not hardly lame. He probably is just busy," Inez remarked. "He does get it in, unlike most niggas. And yeah he does have a work phone but aint no need for me to have that number."

"Well look ... I'm gon leave you with your daughter and bring you some food," the kidnapper said. "Don't you gotta work?"

"Yeah."

"What's the number?"

Silence.

"Either you wanna call off, or not, it's up to you," he pleaded. "I'm just tryna help."

Honestly, he was. He liked Inez, her spunk, her poise. He could tell she was afraid, but she was strong. She didn't want to show them her fear.

"536-6143," said Inez.

The phone rang.

Hello, Meadow Wood Hospice, this is Kathy, can I help you?"

The kidnapper listened first, then put the phone to Inez's ear.

"Kathy?"

"Yes."

"This is Inez," she said into the phone. "I don't think I can make it. Sorry for calling so late but my daughter's sick again and—"

The kidnapper raised his finger and wiggled it from left to right.

"My daughter's doing terrible. I'll do a double next week if you need me to—"

"Nope, that's okay sweetie. You take care of that gorgeous little girl. I'll cover for ya"

"Thank you so much Kathy."

The kidnapper snatched the phone from her and hung up.

"Now try Malik again," said the kidnapper.

Inez had a better idea but she called Malik first like she was asked. Again, his phone went straight to voicemail.

"Why don't you let me call his dude?" she asked. "Maybe I can get a hold of him that way."

The kidnapper was surprised he didn't think of it. He was also surprised she could think under such pressure. Why wasn't she Malik's girl. Then he thought of the girl he saw Malik with the other night. Couldn't lose with either one, he thought.

"Go head," he said.

Inez called L, praying his number was the same. The phone rang. Inez was hopeful.

"He-llo," said L.

Yes, she thought.

"Um, L?"

"Who dis?"

"This is Inez"

"Malik's."

"Yes," said Inez. "Um it's like really, really, really important that I get in contact with him right now. I was hoping."

Inez's voice cracked. She began to cry softly, trying to keep her composure. L noticed the emotion. He feared a relevant thought.

"It aint the baby, is it," L asked. "Is Deja cool?"

The kidnapper couldn't hear what was said on the other line.

"No," said Inez. "But I gotta talk to Malik. Do you have another number I can call?"

"Man hell yeah," L said. "I'm bout to call him on my other phone, hold on."

As L dialed the number the kidnapper became impatient and uncomfortable in his ski mask.

"What he say?" he asked.

"He's calling him on his other phone."

"Good, now when he get on the line you tell him, you need to call him right now!"

"Okaaay leave me alone."

L heard Inez whining.

"Who you talkin to Inez?" asked L.

"Aye, Malik," L said into the phone. "Inez on the other line bro. She said something wrong with the baby. Cut your phone-huh?

"Yeah-yeah-alright," L hung up with Malik.

"Inez?"

"Yes"

"He said call him right now."

*

"I don't know what I'm gonna do," said Jennifer. I consider Melissa a friend. She—"

"You shouldn't have been trying to be so sneaky in the first place," said Toni. "What do you think Malik is going to say the first time he sees you two together."

"I don't know," Jennifer answered honestly.

"I'll tell you what," said Toni. "He's gonna look at you like you're a fuckin psycho."

"Well how am I gonna just stop being Melissa's friend," asked Jennifer. "She likes me. We're cool. He's gonna just have to accept that he's a whore, and Toledo's too small for him to be tryna be all player and shit."

A lot of thoughts raced through Toni's brain. In a way, her sister was right. Then again, Jennifer knew who Melissa was, and she infiltrated her life, with wicked intentions in mind.

"Well I hope you're not thinking of telling Melissa what happened between you and Malik," said Toni.

"Maybe, why?"

"Because that's lame dude, and you know it," her sister said. "Just shut up. You're pissing me off right now."

"Sounds to me like you're on his side," Jennifer laughed.

"I am. The shit you're on—man I've never seen you act like this," said Toni.

"Ugh, I know," Jennifer said. "I wanna fuckin be her. Shit—to tell the truth, I kinda want em both. I'm not gonna be cruel, but I am still gonna be Melissa's friend. I'll keep quiet if he can."

Jennifer's phone rang.

"Hello?"

Silence.

"Hello?"

Click.

"Asshole," Jennifer said unto the phone.

"Who was that?"

"Some dick."

Jennifer's phone rang again this time she looked at the caller I.D. first. It was Melissa.

"Hey Mel."

Melissa was still in a state of disbelief, and more of an emotional wreck after hearing about Malik's problems. She couldn't function properly. Melissa needed someone's shoulder.

"Hi," Melissa spoke. "Um, are you busy?"

"Are you crying," asked Jennifer. "Is everything okay Mel?

"Well—no not really. Can you come over? I'm really."

"Sure I can honey. Where are you?"

"I'm over my boyfriends' house off of Douglas, on Whiteway."

"I'll call you when I'm outside."

"Okay."

Melissa hung up quietly sobbing.

Toni looked at Jennifer waiting to hear about what was going on.

"That was Melissa," said Jennifer.

"See!"

"Yeah, I know. She's like having a crisis or something. She was crying."

"Sounds serious, Jen. If you can't be supportive without plotting you shouldn't go."

"She sounded really hurt. I don't think I could if I wanted to."

"Good."

"You wanna know the crazy part though?" Jennifer asked out loud.

"What?"

"She's over Malik's."

"You're kidding right?" Toni blasted.

"Nope, off of Kenwood," she said. "On Whiteway."

"Damn, is he there?"

"I'm not sure."

Jennifer's phone rang again, and again she checked her identification. It was private. She wasn't going to answer it, but too much was going on at the moment.

"Hello," she answered.

Silence. Jennifer couldn't hear anything on the other end.

"Helloooo."

Click.

"Oh my fuckin goodness! What the hell man."

"Girl you got a lot of drama in your life. Stay a-way." Toni put her fingers together to create a cross, hissing at her sister. "You should go. And don't be a bitch either."

"I'm going."

Jennifer got dressed. She put on a basic Nike jogging suit. White and blue stretch pants, and a blue Nike jacket. She jumped into her car, adjusted the mirror and pulled off. A gray Trail Blazer pulled off after her. The gray truck emulated Jennifer's every move. She was totally unaware of the vehicle behind her, making every turn she made, and stopping at every traffic light. As Jennifer pulled up to the address, Malik pulled off. He didn't notice her, or the Trail Blazer following after him now.

Melissa walked to the door somber and slowly, dressed in pajama pants, and one of Malik sweatshirts. She peered through the peek hole, just as Malik ordered her to do. No one else was allowed over except her friend. Not even the pizza man. Melissa opened the door.

"Poor baby what's wrong," asked Jennifer.

At first sight she could tell Melissa was going through something serious. Jennifer hugged her immediately.

"My best friend—she—she ... she didn't—her boyfriend killed."

Melissa broke down again. Surprisingly, she was able to tell Jennifer what happened. She didn't mention Malik's problems. It seemed like her whole universe was melting in front of her eyes. Melissa was at a loss for words. She was confused. She didn't know what to do or how to do it. She just wanted to be held, not to be alone. Melissa would rather Malik be the one comforting her, but his heart was missing. She couldn't possibly ask him not to go get his child from a kidnapper. What scared her the most was the ice in his eyes. She'd never seen that look before. It was pure, devilish rage.

*

The Trail Blazer followed behind Malik for a half hour. Unknown to the driver, both Malik pit stops were worth fifty thousand a piece. Had the driver known, he would have jumped out right then and there. However, Malik walked into each house with nothing, and appeared to leave with nothing.

The driver decided to follow him a while longer. He knew he was up to something, but time would tell. The driver fell back.

CHAPTER 11

"Tony man, deez niggas is bugging. They got Deja and Inez," Malik said. "They think I'm deer meat, bro. It aint going down like this, on erythang I'm sending these niggas home bro."

"Well what you need me to do bro, I'm ridin," said Tony. "Aint no way I'm a let you ride solo."

"Naw, this what's up. The niggas want me to take the bread to somewhere on Bancroft. They aint told me yet. They say as soon as they see the cash they'll let my daughter go."

"So how you tryna freak it?"

"I figure they going end up doing some predictable shit to make me feel comfortable. Inez and my shorty gon be visible and as soon as they get theirs I'ma get mine," said Malik. "But trick no good. I gotta have that ass."

Malik gave Tony the blueprint In person. The two waited together for the phone call. It took approximately two and a half hours for the kidnappers to call back.

"Alright, look we goin to want you on Lawton," the man on the other line said. "You know where that's at?"

"Yeah, which end?"

"The one closest to the expressway. You'll see us."

"Where my daughter and Inez?"

"Yeah alright," the kidnapper passed the phone to Inez.

"Malik," said Inez. "Please hurry up baby. Deez niggas on some foul shit and I wanna go home."

"How the baby doing?" asked Malik.

"She's fine."

"Did they hurt?"

"That's enough nigga," the kidnapper said. "You got the directions player. Get here."

"I'm on the way."

Malik told Tony what was going on. They fine-tuned their plan. Malik grabbed his snub nose .357 magnum and his .40 cal Smith & Wesson, and a couple of extra clips. Tony brought his Desert Eagle with extra clips and something else a bit heavier, just in case they were outgunned. Tony left first to position himself, hoping he'd get the chance to show the importance of the element of surprise.

Pulling into traffic Malik was more alert than ever. He paid attention to every car that pulled along the side of him, and every set of headlights behind him. Malik thought the same set of headlights had been following him since Douglas. He decided to take a detour down a side street off of Monroe. He turned right, turned off his lights, and parked gripping the magnum. The same headlights turned and pulled up behind him.

The Trailblazer's lights didn't cut off. They shined brightly into the Kia rental Malik was driving. Suddenly, the Trailblazer pulled up on the side of the Kia, and rolled down his window.

"Malik," the driver yelled.

Malik reclined the front seat all the way to the back. The driver looked into the Kia, gun drawn. He couldn't see Malik. The driver was frustrated, he was about to pull the trigger but a car turned down the street in front of him. The driver sped off. Malik heard him scratch out. He leaned to the side and peeked out just to make sure he was gone. Once Malik realized the suspect left he sped off.

"What the fuck," Malik said to himself. "I gotta get outta here."

*

"I'm not doin nothing," Inez said irate.

"I'm sayin baby, that nigga don't want you and I."

"What the fuck make you think I'm gon suck your dick, stupid. I would earl all over the place. You got some muthafuckin nerve."

"Bitch cuz I'm the nigga with the gun," he said.

Inez began to panic. Why would he wait, all this time to flip out? Was he going to kill her anyway, or did he just want to take her sex. Inez directed his attention towards something else.

"Wait, tell me what you got against my child's father?" asked Inez. "I mean, for as long as I've known him, he's been a fair dude, even when he had every reason not to be. I mean, what he do to you."

The kidnapper laughed.

"To tell the truth, he's just a target to me," the kidnapper replied. "I kind of like the nigga after watchin him for the past couple of weeks. But my dude on the other hand really aint feelin ole Malik. So, I guess he gotta get his issue."

"What you mean by that?" Inez asked. "And, why yo dude fag ass always downstairs?"

Silence filled the room. Deja began to make baby noises, as the kidnapper gathered his thoughts.

"We've talked enough, conversation over, Katie Couric."

"Do I know him," Inez paused, actually expecting an answer.

The kidnapper left out the room.

"I must know him," she thought.

Inez sat in the poorly lit room, wondering how many haters Malik actually had. Who was it that linked them both together? Would she ever find out? Will this person continue to be in their lives after all of this is over? Will the masked man remember what was on his mind a few minutes ago demanding sex?

Inez's thoughts were everywhere. She feared for her life. She wondered if she would become a part of the mess that engulfed the room. What about Deja? Would they be so cold as to hurt a small child? Where was Malik? What was taking him so long? Inez began to devise a plan of her own. She couldn't just sit back and wait for someone to harm her or her child. She thought about her options, which were little to none. She thought about the avenue the masked man just gave her. A man always thought with his dick. This one proved he was no different. She thought, even if she got passed him, what about the one downsta

*

"Melissa, where are you?" asked Troy.

"Why?" she said.

"Cuz I need to talk to you in person," he said. "I swear I didn't do that to Jessi."

"Yeah right," said Melissa. "How you aint answer your phone or come to the hospital at all. You think I'm stupid nigga."

"I know you're not stupid Mel, but I can't go to jail for something I didn't do," said Troy. "You know I loved that woman with all I had."

"Tell it to the judge bitch," she yelled. "Ooh I hope you die bitch!"

Click.

Melissa laid in Jennifer's lap. Jennifer stroked her hair trying to comfort Melissa. Melissa had bags under her eyes, wads of tissue cluttered the table in front of her. Her mind was blank. She couldn't think. Her mind wandered back and forth, from Malik and his daughter, back to Jessica. Now Troy was calling. What could he possibly want? He had a lot of nerve, thought Melissa. He sounded desperate to her. Then again he was. His life was definitely on the line.

"Who was that?" asked Jennifer.

"Jessi's murderer," Melissa said flatly.

"What da fuck did he want?"

"I don't know. Trying to explain himself I guess. He wanted to know where I was, which was more bullshit."

"Melissa I'm so sorry you have to go through this. People are so fucked," said Jennifer. "You should see how many x-rays I do a week on abused women. Now I can't lie. Some of those women probably provoke the shit and ask for it, which I never understood. But more often than not, the men do the shit out of frustration, insecurity, and jealousy. Then, amazingly, one—two months down the line, the same woman is back again."

"I know. I should've known something was going on. Jessi never."

"Mel, there's no way you're responsible for any of it."

"I know—I just never knew he was such a coward. They used to be so hap … ."

Both Melissa and Jennifer jumped at the sound of someone knocking on the door.

"Who is that?" asked Jennifer.

Melissa shrugged her shoulders as she slowly rose from the couch tiptoeing towards the door. She looked out the peek-hole. Her heart felt like it would leap from her chest. She ran back to the couch. Both hands covered her mouth.

"Oh my God," Melissa whispered. "It's Troy. He's at the fuckin door."

"What!" Jennifer said in a loud whisper.

"What do we do?" asked Melissa.

"We call the police."

"Okay."

Melissa grabbed Jennifer's hand and powerwalked to Malik's bedroom.

Boom! Boom! Boom!

The knocks were louder and more persistent.

"Hello 9-1-1 emergency. Is this an emergency?" asked the operator.

"Yes!" Melissa continued to whisper. "The man that I think killed my girlfriend is banging at the front door."

"I don't understand," said the operator.

"What's not to understand," said Melissa. "I think a killer is at my front door. He knows I was the last person to see him with my friend before she died."

"Oh, I'm sorry—okay. What's the address ma'am?"

"Twenty-seven thirty-one, Whiteway."

"Did he threaten you in any kind of way or."

"No, but he just called me a few minutes ago before he just showed up uninvited."

"Is he still at the door ma'am?"

"Yes...I think so."

Melissa peeked out of the blinds to see if his car was outside. It was too dark. She couldn't tell. The knocking stopped. Melissa walked back out to the front door to see if he was still there. She and Jennifer crept to the door still gripping each other hand.

"Ma'am," asked the operator.

"I'm checking," said Melissa.

She put her face to the peek-hole. No one stood in front of the door. Melissa searched the hallway with her right eye for a brief second to be sure. She turned around to head back to the couch when she heard it.

BOOM!

Wood chips flew from the doorway. Troy tried to kick the door open in an unsuccessful attempt.

"Ahhh," Melissa and Jennifer screamed. "Please hurry he's trying to shoot the lock off the door. Please hurry"

"Ma'am is there a window you can escape from quickly," asked the operator. "I have units in route right now, but if you can leave."

BOOM!

Another shotgun blast ripped through the lock. Troy kicked the door again. This time he was successful. At first glance no one appeared to be home. Troy stepped inside.

*

"Bitch, come on, and hurry the fuck up," the kidnapper said. "I guess this nigga love ya'll after all."

Inez picked up Dejanique, and held her tight against her chest. The kidnapper grabbed her by her right bicep forcing her down the stairs as if he were recovering her from an extraction point.

The kidnappers didn't tie the blindfold around Inez's eyes in their haste. When they reached the bottom of the stairs she realized she was in a dilapidated crack house. The smell in the basement was unbearable. Inez gagged at the thickness of the stench of urine. She was surprised to see that no one was in the house.

Inez was led out of the back of the house. The kidnapper damn near dragged her to the back porch. She could see a pair of headlights about forty yards down the alley, but they made her and Deja stand handcuffed to the bars on the back door.

"Wait here," said the kidnapper.

He walked towards Malik, stopping halfway in between the Aviator and Malik's Impala, staring at Malik sitting on the hood of the car with a duffel bag next to him. He couldn't quite see the features of Malik's face. Somehow, the kidnapper could see the fire and the malice in his eyes. The kidnapper brandished his weapon.

Malik left his phone on, so Tony could hear what was happening. To be sure Tony heard, Malik repeated what was said.

"Let you get this?" asked Malik. "Nah bring me my family dude. They aint doin nobody no good back there."

The kidnapper looked back towards the truck, nodded his head at Malik. Inez and Deja fidgeted at the door, struggling to shake loose. Malik was ready to kill.

"Ahhhhhhh! Let us go," screamed Inez.

"Aye calm your bitch down dog, "the kidnapper said.

"Inez chill out," yelled Malik.

"You know the drill homie," the kidnapper said. "Same time."

Malik turned around to grab the Jordan bag full of money. As he turned he spoke to Tony on the other end of his watch phone.

"They at the back door of that green house, bro go get em now," said Malik.

Malik turned back around pretending to make sure everything in the bag was in order.

"We good, my nigga," asked the kidnapper.

"I'm just making sure everything is everything," said Malik.

"Yeah, you should."

Malik tossed the bag about fifty feet in front of the kidnapper.

"Now gimme mine," said Malik.

Nobody moved.

*

Tony looked at each house impatiently, trying to get to the right house. Finally, he reached the worn light green house with the unsteady foundation.

"Inez," Tony whispered. "Inez."

Nobody answered. He continued to the back of the house.

"Inez."

Inez jumped at the sound of her name. She thought she'd heard it just seconds before but she thought she was losing it. Now she worried it was one of the kidnappers coming back to harm her.

"Who is that," asked Inez. "Leave us alone."

Inez was ecstatic to see Tony.

"Shhh, be quiet don't even look this way. What are you tied up with," asked Tony crouching with his back rested on the side of the house.

"Fuckin handcuffs," Inez whispered.

"Fuck!"

"Just take the baby, I'm holding her. She aint attached to anything," said Inez.

*

Deja began to cry.

"Damn there go that plan," thought Malik.

The kidnapper talking to Malik snapped his neck towards Inez. He saw someone running. Inez stood out in the open with no baby. He raised his gun.

Blocka! Blocka! Blocka!

Malik fired in the kidnappers' direction. Malik put him on his heels. The kidnapper hid behind the door of the Expedition. The second kidnapper ran for cover as soon as he heard the shots, but now he was taking aim at Inez from behind the SUV. Pop, pop, pop. Inez's body crumbled.

Tony ran from the other side of the house. Pop, pop. He put one in the shoulder and one in lower abdomen of the kidnapper behind the truck.

Malik fired at the door of the truck four more times. The kidnapper tried to retreat from his position, but Malik walked him down. The kidnapper fired backwards without looking. Malik ducked and stopped at the grill of the truck.

The kidnapper crawled away from Malik and right onto the feet of Tony.

"Bro I got em. Come on I got em."

Malik walked around the door and saw the masked man on his hands and knees frozen in fear.

"Where the other one at?" asked Malik.

"Right here."

Malik witnessed the other masked man's saturated shirt. He kept his gun trained on the man on his knees.

"Get up," commanded Malik. "Both of ya'll."

They did as they were told. Tony had already relieved the injured kidnapper of his weapon. Malik did the same to the other one.

"Tony go get my daughter and Inez please."

Tony looked at Malik. He knew Malik must not have seen her fall to the ground. Whatever he did, he knew he had to do it fast.

"Now take them masks off pussies," said Malik.

*

Jennifer pushed Melissa out of one of the bedroom windows. Luckily, Malik stayed on the first floor. Melissa landed on her feet. She quickly reached for her friend, pulling Jennifer through. Another shot was fired inside the apartment. The buckshot's missed its target, but shards of glass from the window stuck into the back of Jennifer's neck.

"Ahhh, ow fuck! My neck," screamed Jennifer.

The two women ran for cover behind a truck parked on the street. Sounds of sirens were heard in the distance. Troy jumped through the window.

"Melissa," said Troy. "This shit aint have nothing to do with you."

Troy cocked the Mossberg 500 pump action shotgun. He slowly crept towards the truck.

Melissa and Jennifer were breathing heavily, but sat in silence trembling with fear. They didn't know what to do next. There was nowhere to go, except open space.

"He's getting closer," whispered Melissa.

She looked underneath the truck and saw Troy walking towards the rear cab of a white F-150.

"You wanna run for it," asked Jennifer. "The sirens are close."

"Yes!"

Without thought, the two women took off in the opposite direction of Troy. Troy rounded the back of the truck, watching the backend of the two women sprinting in full stride. They were at least two car lengths ahead of him. Just as he aimed for Melissa's body, three police cars turned down the street, driving directly into the action. Troy didn't even blink. He squeezed the trigger.

BOOM!

The tires of the squad cars screeched to a halt. Officers jumped out of their vehicles, weapons, drawn, ready to shoot.

"Put the weapon down," yelled an officer.

Another officer ran to the women. One was on the ground. The officer helped Melissa to a sitting position.

"Ma'am, are you okay," asked the officer.

"Ah! Yeah I'm fine it just stings a little."

The officer looked at her bleeding leg.

"Looks like it was only a couple of buckshot's," said the officer. "You should be alright when the—"

"Put the fucking gun down," yelled a fellow officer.

Troy looked around. More police were showing up by the second. He slowly lowered the gun, but within a split second he turned the barrel on himself.

"Nooo! Sir we can work."

BOOM!

CHAPTER 12

"What the fuck is your name?" Malik demanded.

"Nigga I aint tellin you shit," said the kidnapper.

Blocka!

Malik shot him in the leg.

"What is it?"

"Fuck you bitch."

Tony pulled up with Deja.

Blocka!

Malik shot him in the shoulder.

"Come on Malik baby. We can't do this here," said Tony. "Inez is hurt bad man. We gotta go."

Malik looked at Tony with pure rage in his eyes. Tony had never seen his friend this upset, even when they had put work in before.

"Ah, ah,sss, ah," screamed the kidnapper. "Ask yo bitch nigga."

"My bitch," asked Malik. "Tony how bad is Inez?"

"She should be cool fam if we get her to the hospital in time. She caught one in the upper thigh."

Whack! Whack! Malik smacked both kidnappers across the face. In his heart of hearts he didn't want to kill the two men, but what else could he do. He couldn't just walk away.

For the heartache they caused both him and his daughter's mom. The stress of looking over his shoulder every day was not an option. What if they pressed charges on him? He'd be damned if he went to jail for fifteen years for some shit they caused.

"God forgive me." Malik raised the .357 to one of their heads.

Flop! One shot rang out. The man crumbled to the gravel.

"Take your mask off."

The kidnapper looked Malik in the eyes.

"It's me man," said the man behind the mask.

Tony snaked his neck around, facing the man. He watched as the injured man slowly took off his mask.

"Hurry up, bitch!" Malik reached over and pulled the mask off.

Tony's face went white.

Malik was so stunned he fell to his knees.

"Sean?"

"Aw naw," said Tony. "What da fuck you on Sean? What da fuck bro—this is my man. You know that."

"I know," whispered Sean as blood trickled out of his mouth. "I got thirsty. Ya'll niggas was eatin—I let this nigga gas me up."

"Aye, I'm a let you handle this one fam," Malik said as if he didn't understand life anymore. "I need to get Inez outta here."

Sean fell over on his side. He needed help bad.

"Naw bro. You know what it is," said Tony. "I know you aint tryna leave it like this."

Tony turned towards his cousin, tears pouring down his face, snot running out of his nose.

BLOU!

Malik helped Tony put the bodies in the kidnappers truck. Tony stared at his cousin briefly before he closed the back door. He felt the worst kind of pain, the kind that wouldn't subside from drinking or taking a Percocet 30.

Malik took Inez to the hospital. He explained he'd be back for her. She'd lost a lot of blood while he and Tony shot it out with her abductors. She didn't want him to go but she knew if she wanted her child's father to be in her life, he needed to leave. She had to suck it up. Malik didn't want to part with his daughter, but he had to for a second to help his man. He thought about keeping her. If anything happened he'd play the daddy role. But the night was so ill he didn't want to chance it. He opted to drop her off at his mother's house. Malik, rushed to a junkyard just outside of the Toledo city limits.

"Why ya'll dumpin this truck," asked Mark.

Mark was a skinny dusty looking white man. He had red curly hair, an unshaven face, wearing a blue flannel jacket.

"Does it matter Mark?" asked Malik.

"Yeah, I might want the motherfucker it's a good truck."

"No, it's not, and it never will be. This is a night I will never forget in life," said Malik. "I'm a burn this bitch up in the middle of all this junk. I need you to let this bitch burn for an hour plus, and compact this muthafucka into a hot wheel. You hear me?"

"Yeah I do, and I'm done asking questions jack. What do I do if … ."

"They won't. Just do it now, right here."

Malik tossed Mark one of the stacks of money that he never planned on giving the kidnappers in the first place. Tony was mute during the whole exchange.

"Nope nothing left to say. Matter of fact … ."

Mark disappeared. Two hours later, Mark sent a picture of the flattened vehicle.

*

"Babe, where are you?" Melissa sounded more alive than she had all day.

"Bout to come home, why?" asked Malik.

"Did everything work out alright?"

"Yeah, but I gotta go check on Inez and the baby," he said. "I don't feel right leaving em by their self. Inez in the hospital, she got shot in the leg."

"Damn," said Melissa. "That's deep. Can you come get me first then?" she asked.

"Why what's wrong?"

Melissa shook her head.

"I hate to stress you baby I swear, just come get me first and then I'll tell you, but we can't stay at your house. I'm at Toledo Hospital."

"Da fuck for," Malik whined.

"Baby calm down," Melissa stressed. "I'm perfectly fine just come get me, but it is some bullshit in the game."

"Who it have to do with," asked Malik. "Just tell me that."

"Troy? Troy who? Jessi's Troy?"

"You would never believe it baby," said Melissa.

"Fuck, fuck, fuck," Malik banged his hands against the steering wheel. "I'm on the way."

"Bro go to your house. I gotta use your car."

Tony took Malik to his truck. Malik called Inez as soon as he started the engine:

"Hello?"

"You alright?" asked Malik.

"I don't know ... no, where are you?"

"You wouldn't believe this shit tonight," said Malik. "But aye, you know I can't be at the spital' with you so dig just hold it down for me babe. You told the hook what I told you to tell em, right?

"Yes. You gonna have the baby right?

"Yea, fa sho," said Malik. "If you need something call Melissa. We gon get it to you."

"Okay, babe. I love you," said Inez, meaning every word of it.

"Love you too."

Malik drove past his apartment. The police were everywhere. It reminded him of the time he pulled up on Rene.

After taking inventory of the scene, Malik sped to the Toledo Hospital. After he packed Malik dialed Melissa's phone number.

"Yeah babe," answered Melissa.

"What room you in?"

"Thirty-six o-seven."

"I'll be up there in a minute."

Malik took the elevator to the third floor. After power walking down the long corridor, Malik walked right into the unlocked room.

The first thing Malik noticed was the ace bandage wrapped around the thigh of Melissa. The second thing he noticed was the familiar smell of Dolce& Gabana. Malik didn't dwell on the fragrance too long, and went to hug and kiss his rib.

"You okay baby? Damn, what the fuck happened?"

Melissa went on to tell the story, but before she got to the part about her great escape, out walked Jennifer. Malik sat paralyzed for a brief moment. He wasn't sure how he should react.

"Sooo ... you must be Jennifer?" asked Malik. "You're who I've been hearing about?"

"I am," said Jennifer. "I've heard so much about you. It's crazy that we had to meet like this."

"Aint it doe,' said Malik. "Babe you gotta stay here for the rest of the night?"

"Naw, I already got my prescription for the pain. Me and my ride or die chick were waiting for you."

Malik laughed.

"You cool?" Malik asked Jennifer.

"Just a couple scrapes from the window, but I'm good, thanks to Malik's Angel over there," said Jennifer.

"Well let's ride. I gotta get my seed," said Malik. "Jennifer you need a ride?"

Jennifer's face flushed. She scratched the back of her scalp.

"Ummm, I do but I don't want to inconvenience you. You must've had one helluva night?"

Malik frowned at Melissa. What did she know about his, life altering night?

"Why you say that?" asked Malik.

"Because Melissa wouldn't call you for shit," Jennifer tried to clean it up. "She thought you were majorly busy. And I'm like look at what just happened ... I just figured—never mind, I'll just call a cab."

"Okay. See you later. Babe let's go," said Malik.

"Malik," yelled Melissa, "After all of this you're going to make her take a cab?"

Malik pulled the truck around to the front where Jennifer waited with Melissa as she sat in her wheelchair. Both women got in.

"You in a rush to get home Jennifer?" asked Malik.

"Strangely, I'm kind of wired. Why?"

"Gotta make a detour. Matter of fact, you've just been kidnapped."

Melissa looked over at Malik uneasily.

"Sorry," said Malik. "But since you part of the family now, you're coming with us."

Malik proceeded to pick up his daughter. He found out Inez would be discharged the next evening. He still had a funny feeling.

*

Roscoe tried to stay incognito, walking along the sidewalks of Ottawa Drive. He knew if he stayed on the main streets police would stop and harass him. After he sped away from Malik, he crashed his vehicle into a telephone pole. The cuts on his neck, and open wound on his forehead were tell-tell signs of an altercation. He cut through Ottawa Park to get to Ottawa Drive. There was an abandoned house boarded up with plywood. It was as good a place as any to avoid going to jail. Roscoe pried open the make shift door, and began preparing his bed for the night.

*

Inez lay in her bed, thinking about the last twenty-four hours. Who were the kidnappers? What did Malik and Tony do to them? Was it all over? Most importantly, where was Malik now?

No sooner than the thought crossed her mind, Inez's phone rang.

"Hello?"

"Open the door, my nig," said Malik.

Inez didn't waste any time. She hung up on Malik without saying a word. Malik helped her to the car but, Inez didn't need any help, nor did she want any. Malik still grabbed her bags and threw them in the trunk. Deja played with her hand in the backseat. Inez snatched her out of her car seat and jumped in the front seat, holding her child as if she'd never let go.

"What took you so long?" asked Inez.

She didn't expect an answer. Her face was twisted in genuine concern. She leaned over the console and kissed Malik, not due to her desire for him, but because she was so frightened, and confused, and grateful, and relieved.

Inez had so many questions. Malik always downplayed any success he's ever had. She was surprised by the amount of money the kidnappers were asking for. She realized she didn't know Malik the way she thought.

"I aint know your mama was coming to pick you up, or else we would've been there," said Malik. "How you doing doe? You straight?"

"I hurt like a muthafucka, but I guess I'm gon be cool. Where are we going?"

"Well dig man … last night was blatant. Melissa got shot yesterday too. I'm too tired to even talk about the shit. But in short we all going be livin together until we work sumthin else out."

"I'm scared Malik," said Inez. "What if it's more niggas involved?"

"It is."

"What you mean by that?" asked Inez.

"I mean some other shit going on and I don't want you or my child near the bullshit."

Inez understood, but her face showed confusion. What did Malik have going on? It all seemed surreal. How did all this happen? Was she responsible? So many questions, so few answers.

"Where are we supposed to go?" asked Inez as a giant tear began to glide down her flushed cheeks.

"I told you, you with me for a while. It don't matter how long," Malik said. "We gonna work it out, but you and Melissa just gonna have to learn to get along. I already talked to her, so it is what it is until shit cool off.

The car grew silent. It had been a long thirty-six hours for the both of them. Malik calculated his next four moves, hoping death or jail wasn't in the equation. Who's that lucky, he thought. He stole a glance at Dejanique. He knew he would protect her at whatever cost, but wasn't she better protected with him around? Malik wasn't a killer, he knew that, but after what happened earlier he felt the ice crystalizing in his veins. His heart beat different. If he had to kill again he knew he would kill again. He didn't want to become that person, but to protect himself and his daughter, there was no question what he'd do.

CHAPTER 13

Tony sat at home lost in his thoughts. He was in disbelief of the previous days' events. He watched his cousins' life spill out of his stomach. Tony was ashamed he hadn't helped him. Sean left him no choice. What was he supposed to do? He felt like he did the right thing for Malik, but not for himself.

Life was strange indeed. For some reason the joys of everyday living never softened the blows of everyday pain. Even though Tony felt the most indescribable hurt, he knew there was no other choice to make. He had to ride it out with Malik, his friend, his brother. If people wanted Malik dead, then fuck it, they must want him out the way too.

Tony hadn't slept all night. He decided to get some rest. He knew if God allowed him to wake in the morning, the pain would still exist.

*

A mouse nibbled at Roscoes' shoe. As he felt the light pressure of the rodent against his sole, he upped pipe so fast he damn near blew his own pinky toe off.

"Fuck," he yelled, wiping the sleep from his eyes.

Noticing the thick dust on the floor, and the thin beams of sun shining through the boarded up windows, he remembered he had to abort the mission last night.

Roscoe sat up, tending to his wounds. He realized he had underestimated his adversary, even though he lucked up. There was a time to retreat, but never surrender.

"Hello?" Roscoe spoke into his phone. "Is this Black and White Cab … It is? Aye, I need a cab to pick me up from the gas station on Monroe and Auburn, and tell the driver to call this number when he gets there."

Roscoe waited for his cab, thinking about how much he hated Malik.

"Let me get all of it then," said Roscoe.

"I can't let you get all of it. I told my dude I'd call him when you left," said James. "That's my nigga I can't leave him dry."

"Naw?" Roscoe pulled his strap. "Let me get all of it then."

James gasped as he eyed the half of kilo of cocaine on the table.

"So that's how you do me," said James. "I feed you, you thirsty ass nigga."

"Look dude jus … ."

"Dude, Malik only playin wit a couple of ounces. I was gonna shoot him a mac and let him work. Just buy the rest and I'll forget the stupid shit you doin right now."

"Nigga I got the upper hand right now—matter of fact … Fuck you nigga!"

BLOU!BLOU!

Roscoe shot James once in the thigh and once in the stomach. He threw the cocaine in a grocery bag and fled through James' backdoor. Just as he was leaving through the back, Malik was walking through the front. He saw James leaking, looking weak.

"What the fuck bruh? You cool," asked Malik.

James pointed towards the back.

"Check back their bro," he said in agonizing pain. "The nigga just left through the back."

Malik pulled out his strap and ran towards the back. He got outside just in time to see Roscoe straightening his car and fleeing down the alley.

Pop, pop, pop.

Malik fired at the back window, blowing it out with his third shot.

Pop, pop, pop.

The car's tire screeched as Roscoe made a sharp right turn, pulling into traffic. As Roscoe avoided Malik, he drew the attention of a squad car due to his reckless driving and blown out back window. The chase was on.

Roscoe had a slight lead on the squad car. As he turned into a neighborhood off of Central and Collingwood, the officer didn't see Roscoe pitch his gun, but he did see him toss the bag of cocaine. As Roscoe was getting rid of the evidence, he didn't notice the cruiser in front of him, positioned to block him off. He slammed on the breaks of the black Mark VII, but not fast enough to stop from slamming into the squad car.

Roscoe's head jammed violently against the steering wheel, knocking him out instantly. The police recovered the drugs, and gun ignorant to the crime he committed just ten minutes earlier.

During his pre-trial, Roscoe knew James would show. But much to his delight James kept it fair. Nobody knew about the felonious assault or robbery except him, James, and Malik, and Malik never saw him.

Roscoe plead to eight years in prison for the drugs and eighteen months for the pistol. His sentence was to be served concurrently, leaving him to do only eight.

Roscoe's phone rang, snapping him out of his daydream, at the bus stop.

"Hello?" said Roscoe.

"Yes this is Black and White. I'm at gas station now."

"Yeah, here I come."

Roscoe never forgot that day. He felt like Malik should have stayed out of the whole situation. When Malik fired those shots, Roscoe panicked. He fled the scene discombobulated, and confused. He didn't see it as karma biting him in the ass for biting the hand that fed him. It was all in the game to him. Roscoe imagined Malik slamming the gavel on him that day in court. He promised himself he would pay Malik back in full.

*

One month later Malik wasn't all that thrilled to have Inez and Melissa under one roof. He enjoyed the time he spent with his daughter, but all the petty little arguments and evil looks was starting to play itself out. Out of the two women's injuries, Inez's had proven to be the worst. Melissa started going back to work, while Inez was at her home playing house with Malik. Malik knew Melissa's patience was wearing thin, so he found a nice spacious two-bedroom apartment where Inez could stay.

"I don't think I'm ready to be on my own Malik," said Inez. "I mean I been cool cuz I've been with you but I'm still shook about that shit for real."

"Yeah, I know," said Malik. "But at the same time how long you think you and baby girl gon keep restraining yourselves. I know it's a helluva situation, but damn I'm a good nigga. I'm doing what I feel like I should do, but I aint going fa no fuck shit between ya'll. Period."

"Mmmhmm, you aint never cater to me like that."

"Oh, that's what we on?" asked Malik. "I thought you was off that. I see you got a lot of growing up to do, my nigga."

"I'm not your nigga."

"Man shut up. Listen I aint trying to go through it with you bout trying to protect you and my seed dude."

"Well I'm just going go back home."

"See that's why we couldn't get along in the first place. You have always been so fuckin stubborn and dumb. You don't think. And where the fuck you think my daughter going be at?"

Silence.

"See what I'm sayin," said Malik. "You just think about what's good for you, you can't even see I'm looking out for your best interest. You act like you don't even respect it."

"I do, I'm just sayin nigga all this shit happened cuz of you. This shit aint cuz of nothing I did."

"Damn, that's how you feel? Man niggas thirsty as fuck. It aint about what I did or nobody else. These busted ass niggas see a nigga getting it and want parts cuz they aint got no work ethic. They only motive is to take sumthin from a nigga cuz they think he got it. But I see how it's laying," said Malik. "Bitch you wasn't trippin before Dejanique got here. You wasn't trippin when you was in the passenger seat makin runs wit me, waking me up talking bout 'your phone ringing' and all that."

"Why you always gotta flip out on me," said Inez. "I'm just hurt Malik this bitch got everything that's supposed to be mine, and kicking me out cuz she said something."

"Dig, you know you aint feeling this situation either. You act like I'm just going leave you stranded and not check on you every chance I get. The shit was fucked up, but let's not forget, I did come to the rescue. I know a lot of mufuckas that would of left their baby's mama right where she was at."

Melissa walked into the argument, already knowing what was going on.

"Ya'll alright in here," said Melissa.

"Yea, we good," said Malik not wanting to discuss it in front of Melissa.

Inez just rolled her eyes.

"Whatever, so when am I moving," said Inez trying to act like a lady in front of one.

"I'll let you know," said Malik.

Inez walked away with a slight limp, actually doing better than what she put on. Melissa kissed Malik and went to the bathroom. Malik sat down, exhausted physically and mentally. This shit was putting too much stress on him. The more he thought about everything. It bothered him, he never found out who tried to get at him before the exchange with Inez and his daughter. There wasn't a day that went by that he didn't try to figure it all out. However, the more he thought about it the more he became confused. He, Tony, and Juan tried to put their heads together but everybody was drawing blanks. They thought about Roscoe. He was the number one suspect, but no one had seen him before the incident or since. Thinking with the mind of a man from the street this was all the more reason to put him on the top of the list. Malik knew he was robbing people, but couldn't understand what drove him to seek Malik out so intently. Either way Malik didn't think he could fall victim to a powder head.

A few weeks later Malik was at Inez's new townhouse. He was there to drop Deja off, but ended up staying to eat a couple of chicken fajitas. Malik's phone made a noise. His battery was low.

"Aye you aint got no house charger for this phone," asked Malik.

"Nope," said Inez.

"Damn," said Malik. "I'll just put it on the car charger. I'll be right back. Make some Kool-Aid."

While he was plugging in his phone he got a text from Juan:

Call other number diff line.

Malik ran back in the house.

"Lemme see yo phone real quick."

He scrolled down to Juan's name forgetting about calling the other phone. Just as he remembered, he stumbled on a name but called Juan first.

"What it do?" said Malik.

"Not shit, just tryna see what's up with the what's up."

"What you mean?"

"When we going on vacation nigga?"

"Damn you right my nigg ... ."

"Yea you forgot, fa self-ass nigga," Juan shook his head.

"Naw I was just letting everything simmer down a little bit."

"I can dig it black. Where you at?"

"B.M."

"Playing wit fire aint you boi. You using that baby daddy card?"

"Ha! Yea right dude. Not today anyway. Aye doe," Malik walked off lowering his voice. "Aint Roscoe real name Jermaine?"

"Yeah I think so. You gotta ask Tone to be sure, but I'm pretty sure it is though. Why?"

"I'm gon call you right back."

"Inez."

Malik jumped as he turned around, not expecting her to be right behind him.

"Dude I'm right here, damn," said Inez.

"Shut up. Who is Jermaine?"

"Why you going through my phone, lame?"

Malik couldn't help but laugh.

"Chill out. Don't flatter yourself too much now," said Malik. "But fa real doe its important. Do he go by Roscoe too?"

Inez looked confused. She picked Deja up out of her walker and sat on the couch.

"Yes—I guess you know him?"

"Has he been to your old spot or anything like that?"

"No."

"When was the last time you talked to him," asked Malik.

"I don't know, a couple-weeks," Inez's voice trailed off as she realized she hadn't talked to him since the day before the kidnapping.

"Have you met him anywhere or told him where you stayed?"

"Yes we kicked it a couple of times. I never told him where I stayed though."

173

"Have you ever been to his crib?"

"Nope."

"Damn you aint no help. I need this number."

"Don't be … ."

"Don't be what? Just shut yo ass up and let me handle this shit. If he call you though tell him you got into it with me and you need to come over."

Malik wrote down the number, kissed his daughter and left.

*

"Ooooooh! Yea…..wait—I can't … I'm bout to."

"Shhhh."

"Oh my God—my pussy is so wet. What are you—ohhhhhh shiiiiiit! Don—don't stop … ."

Toni gripped the black satin sheets on her bed, as she squatted on all fours. Her ass was high in the air, gripped by a set of manicured hands. A different body lay underneath Toni. The body was shining with sweat, long and sexy, bronze skin with no pubic hair.

The woman underneath Toni sucked at her clit, slurped up all of her juices, and slipped her tongue inside Toni's box.

"Ooooh, shit. Got damn your tongue! Oh my God! I'm….I."

Alana slid her wet middle finger inside Toni's ass. Her tone changed. It was more commanding. She rode the tip of

Alana's finger and her face simultaneously at a pace only lust could provide.

"You like that?" asked Alana.

"Oooh, hell yea," Toni whimpered. "Fuck me me....oooh fuck me, ahhhh yes."

Alana penetrated her slightly deeper.

"I'm coming—I'm coming—I'm coming……shiiiiit."

"Ride—my—face. Get it baby, get it."

Alana thrust her lizard-like tongue into the air, allowing Toni to brush back and forth across the tip, stimulating her clit, her lips, and her opening with each stroke.

Toni closed her eyes, clenched the satin in her tight fists.

"I'm gonna cuuuuum."

Her body jerked wildly, as her face contorted into a look she would never be able to duplicate. Toni's lustful fluids squirted from her body. Alana pushed Toni onto her back, massaging her pearl frantically, taking her to a completely different level of orgasm, as she continued to shoot long streams of cum across the bed.

"I'm gonna fuck you so good," said Toni.

"Yeah," smiled Alana. "So you like?"

"Wow! That would be an understatement. Although, you made me think about someone."

Alana's face twisted involuntarily.

"So I give you damn near the whole nine yards and you thinking about somebody else?"

"Yeah, but not how you think. See there's this man I."

"I don't—Its not that I don't like dick, because I do. But a lot of times in these situations that I'm sure you're about to propose, almost always go sour."

"Listen I'm not going to lie to you, I'm gambling. Never had sex with this man ever, but for some reason I just want to please him," said Toni. "I'm so confident that he'll deliver for the both of us, I'll be your personal slave for one whole month if he doesn't and that's not just limited to sex."

"What? How can you be so sure about somebody you've never had?

"I don't know. Guess I can't. But the catch to the bet is this, if he does perform for us, you'll do *my* bidding for a month," Toni sat back with a smug look on her face.

"Call him."

Toni called promptly.

"Hello?" answered Malik.

"Hi," said Toni. "Wutcha doing?"

Malik laughed.

"Just tryna wrap my mind around some other shit," said Malik. "But you sound like you up to no good. What you want?"

"I just haven't talked to you in a while that's all. Is that cool?"

"I'm good—I guess."

"Why you say it like that? You need some company or something?"

"No reason, just trying to figure out what you up to. As far as company go, tell the truth I wouldn't mind. I need a crucial body rub. Can you handle that?"

"Definitely, are you stopping by?"

"Yeah, gimme a minute."

"Alright don't be playing. If you do it's your loss."

"Don't hype me up. You better be talking bout something."

"Oh, I'm gonna deliver."

Malik thought about it for a second.

"Damn I aint shit," Malik mumbled.

"What?"

"Nothin, I'm on the way."

CHAPTER 14

Malik sat outside of Toni's home tearing open a box of Trojans. He stuffed the three condoms into his pocket, and littered in the street. Malik pulled out his phone.

"Sup bro?" Tony asked.

"Aye call me in exactly an hour and a half."

"Fuckin wit them hoes again, aint cha boy."

Malik laughed.

"Stay out my business dude. Nosey mufucka. One hour, *thirty minutes.*"

"Turn me on or I aint doin shit," said Tony.

Malik laughed again.

"Lame ass dude. Peace! Don't forget."

"Peace!"

Malik called Toni.

"Hello?" answered Toni.

"Open the doe," said Malik.

Malik walked towards the house as the garage door opened. He entered the house, immediately making himself at home, making his way to the basement. Malik realized he'd never seen the basement before.

The basement was nice. The furniture, carpet, and walls all coordinated in an array of cream and tan. When Malik saw the 50" flat on the wall, he laughed to himself.

"What deez hoes been on extreme makeover or sumthin," he thought.

Malik noticed a mini-bar against the wall. He helped himself to a drink, clicked on the screen, and put his feet up. Malik was startled by the honey colored woman standing in front of him. He quickly noticed after assessing her from head to toe. Shorty was the shit.

"Nuh uh," she said. "Damn, you just chillin huh?"

She was definitely mixed with something.

"What you mixed with?" asked Malik.

The girl smiled.

"No introduction or nothing, just straight to it."

"Well that was the first question that came to my mind."

"What do you think?"

"Hmmm, maybe some type of Latin heritage," Malik tilted his head, studying her features. "Nice lips, smooth creamy skin, wavy hair, light eyes, edible body—I mean adequate body—some type of island. Fuck it I don't know, Hawaiian and South American."

Her smile was wider this time, standing with both hands on her lower back.

"Is that your fantasy woman, Malik?"

"One of them."

"Damn, at least you're honest."

"I am."

"Mmmhmm," caramel folded her arms across her chest.

"What?" asked Malik.

"Nothin, well sorry to disappoint you sir, but I'm merely a poor Trinidad girl with a White father."

It was Malik's turn to smile.

"It's still interesting to me. I'm just a regular ole black person," he said.

She burst out into laughter. Malik sipped his vodka.

"I'm Alana by the way."

"O my fault, I'm Malik."

They extended their hands simultaneously.

"I know who you are dude."

"So, you just gon stand there the whole time? I aint gon snatch you up," said Malik as cool as he could, catching on slowly.

Alana raised her eyebrows and shrugged her shoulders.

"I aint never scared nic-ca."

She sashayed her way next to Malik on the sectional. Alana's nostrils were immediately flooded with the scent of Dolce & Gabana. A nice treat, she thought, as she crossed her legs, and arms. Alana began to bounce the left leg over her right one.

"So, you stay here by yourself?" asked Malik.

"Cute."

"Not that I mind your company."

"Toni's in the shower. I can go get her."

"Naw you cool. I was just fuckin with you," said Malik. "But fa real, how you know Toni? I aint never seen you before."

Malik wasn't looking at her gorgeous face as he spoke. Alana's thick thigh had the man mesmerized. She noticed.

"I'm new," Alana stated plainly, playing along, placing her hand between her thighs. Malik looked up momentarily, stealing a glance at Alana's features, watching for any weakness. She held steady.

"Dig that. So, what makes you so special that you get a free run at the crib? What you bringing to the table? I know Toni don't fuck with too many people. So, I'm guessing you must be an exceptional individual."

Alana put her knees up on the couch, her elbow sat on the headrest, hand on her cheek, turning towards Malik.

"What do you bring Mr. Malik?"

"I bring peace, tranquility, reliability, and trust. I'm not boasting, but I just think I'm loved because I'm me all the time, and being me is not similar to being anyone else."

"Oh—I see. Well that's a tough act to follow. I bring joy Malik, and pleasure, and fun, and spontaneity," said Alana. "Is that an asset to you?"

"Absolutely—after all the pain in the world we gotta learn to appreciate joy, and pleasure, and fun."

"How so?" asked Alana.

Malik just stared at her. He knew he was about to go in. His silence was the loudest thing in the room. The conversation had gotten predictable. The game was on.

Malik grabbed Alana's hand, pulling her towards him.

"What are you doing?" she asked.

He didn't speak. He continued pulling her closer. She resisted slightly, but Malik's strength insisted an inch further. Alana submitted. Her body went limp. This game they played excited her mentally and physically. So, far, Malik was the aggressor. Her body heat told her she was pleased by his assertiveness if nothing else.

A kiss on her neck weakened Alana even more, then came another and another. When Malik's tongue engaged Alana's flesh, she resigned with the moment. Malik's hands wasted no time reaching Alana's hair, latching on tugging aggressively. He lifted Alana's tank top with his other hand, exposing her breast, and her golden brown nipples.

"Mmmm," moaned Alana as Malik put his mouth on her.

Alana was temporarily distracted by Malik's mouth when he freed his hand and dipped his finger in between her juicy lips.

"Sssss," Alana sucked in her breath at the unexpected.

Malik couldn't believe how smooth she was. He stole some of her honey and used it to massage her pearl. Malik kissed Alana in the mouth, massaging her pussy, creating a flash flood between her legs.

Alana wanted to make him come fast at first. Now all she wanted was Malik inside of her. Malik wasn't finished. He pulled her shorts off, undressing himself at the same time, laying himself on top of her. He slid himself back and forth across her pearl, while he fondled, and kissed and caressed her body.

"Damn—oooh shit what are you doing," asked Alana.

Malik could see how bad she wanted him. He could feel how wet she was becoming. The allure of teasing Alana made him more aggressive towards his goal.

"Please put it in—mmm Malik," whispered Alana. "Why are you playing with me? C'mon"

"Okay," stated Malik.

He dove into her ocean face first.

"Ohhh—mmmmmm—yesss—damn –ssssss –damn your tongue—feels –oh shit—oooo."

Alana's legs were already shaking, but she was only experiencing small quakes. Malik knew she'd explode quickly, so instead of going hard for the next sixty seconds, Malik cruelly spelled his name in cursive, slow, and intently for the next sixty.

"Malik, oh my God, she was righ—righ—right. I'm about to … ."

As soon as Alana tried to warn Malik her orgasm was coming, he stopped, made sure the rubber was on, and plunged into her body. Alana's back arched as if her body was being invaded by a spiritual entity. Malik had no mercy. He stretched her walls and touched the bottom of her canal, sliding in and out like a piston with purpose, intensity, and precision. He pulled her hair again, and palmed her ass, pulling her onto every inch of him.

"Fuck ahhh—ah—ahhhh—mmmmm—oh shit—sssss, motherfucker you better not take it out."

Alana locked her legs around Malik's back.

"Ho-ly shiiiiiit ahhh," Alana screamed.

Her body jerked and twitched uncontrollably for over a minute.

"My turn."

Both Malik and Alana turned towards the television. Toni stood there in her birthday suit, walked closer. She pulled Malik out of Alana, pushed him on his back, pulled off the condom, and sucked him into her mouth. Toni quickly rolled another condom over Malik's erection, and slid down his sex as if she were savoring every inch he had to offer.

"Mmmmhmmm," Toni rocked her hips. "ahhhh— now—mmm—make—uh—ah—oooooh, damn, make me feel like her."

*

On the other side of the city someone got their rocks off in a different way.

"Gimme a light," demanded Roscoe.

"Go," yelled his new partner Smitty.

A tow-truck lowered its bed right through the windows of Malik's Barbershop. After the glass shattered, Roscoe threw three Molotov cocktails into the shop. He and his new best friend got to the car just in time to see how much damage they were causing. The whole shop was engulfed in flames that fast. Roscoe took pride in his work, but for some reason, he didn't feel as good as he thought he would. This will definitely bring Malik out of hiding, thought Roscoe.

Even though he was second guessing his self, Roscoe wasn't sure if he was going about the situation the proper way. His face twisted with concern as he fired up a Salem 100.

"This dude Smitty," Roscoe blew out his smoke. "He so arrogant, think he can't be touched. He prolly don't even remember how he fucked me over. Maybe I should just tell him to pay me and I'll let him live."

Smitty was blacker than tar, almost a deep purple. His face was fat, and the whites of his eyes glowed in the dark. His short nappy afro looked neat behind the sharp lining that outlined his coif.

"I don't know fam. I heard niggaz put him through it not too long ago," said Smitty. "But aint nobody seen or heard from them boys since. The nigga is not a fool, feel me? I say go at him like you going at him, bring to the front, but once you

185

bring him to the front you gotta be prepared to lay him out where he stand, if you not … think of another plan."

Roscoe looked over at Smitty.

"Think so?"

"Fa sho."

*

"Damn," Malik was out of breath stroking Toni from the back. "This some bomb ass pussy. Ya'll so scandalous."

He continued to give Toni the business, pushing her ass upwards, spreading her cheeks, plowing deeply into her body.

"Oh shit, oh shit—"Toni cried.

"Fuck I'm bout to cum—I-I can't."

"Don't hold back baby cum with meee—ah."

"Aww shiiiit—mutha—fuck—mmmmmmm-um—mmm."

Malik froze inside of Toni. She continued to roll her hips. Making Malik jerk and twitch. Alana sat her sexy ass in between Toni and Malik. Alana pulled the rubber off of Malik's still hard dick, and put it in her mouth.

"Whose head is better?" asked Alana as she practically swallowed Malik's man-hood. "Me—um—or—" Alana took it out of her mouth held it in her hand passing it to Toni.

"Oh my God," said Malik as Toni licked him from balls to head. "Where the fuck am I? Whew shit."

Just as he was judging the best contest he'd ever been a part of, the phone rang, and rang, and rang. Malik was oblivious to any sounds or anything going on around him except for the two women.

*

"How dis nigga gon … ," Tony pressed the end button, then pressed send.

"Mutha fucka answer the phone."

On the fifth ring he picked up.

"Hello?" answered Malik.

"Nigga you aint done yet?"

"Not necessarily."

"Well dig this, my dude."

"Ahhhh shit—wait, wait, wait," Malik said.

"Damn it's going down like that?" Tony asked.

"Good lookin bro, but I'm going to need some more time in the booth."

"Well do your one-two my dude. I did my part I'm goin to bed."

"I'm a call you when I leave," whispered Malik.

"Yeah."

Tony hung up and walked into his kitchen. Rene admired his shirtless body from the couch.

"Babe," Rene yelled.

"Wut up doe?"

"Let's do some shots."

Tony eyed his fiancé strangely.

"You wanna go out?"

"Naw—I mean right now—right here."

"Is that right?" Tony smirked.

"Yup."

"Vodka or Cognac?" Tony questioned.

"Patron or Cuevo," Rene' shot back.

"Oh you feelin like that? Well I'm gon grab the salt and the lemons. You pick, bartender."

CHAPTER 15

"What the fuck," Malik mumbled.

He stood in front of his barbershop. His black Chicago White Sox hat pulled down over his eyes, broke to the left. He wore a gray Artful Dodger hoody over his hat, black jeans, and black and gray Rockport's. The color of his outfit definitely depicted his mood. Standing there, Malik was shocked; traumatized as if he couldn't understand the scenery in front of him. Malik didn't speak. He didn't move. His eyes didn't blink. The frustration showed. Why was this happening he wondered?

Melissa was calling.

"Sup babe?" asked Malik.

Melissa could hear the hurt in his tone. She heard exhaustion, rage, aggravation, and guilt. She asked herself why would she hear guilt mixed along with these emotions. Her alarm went off.

"Baby what's the matter?" Melissa asked.

"Man. You not gon' believe this one here."

"What? ... Try me?

"I'm standing in front of my shop and it has been blown up. It's still burning right now."

"What! What do you mean blown up?"

"I mean somebody rigged some shit up or somethin and made my shop a thing of the past," he said.

"Oh baby, I'm sorry. Do you want me to come?"

"Naw babe I'm going holler at da hook for a minute and I'll be home in about an hour I guess."

"Okay. Baby I love you."

"Love you too."

On the drive home, Malik was exhausted and confused. The sex-capade he just had felt like a fond memory at best. Thoughts in his brain were piling up together like a terrible wreck on I-75. He thought an ability to think straight would be priceless at the moment.

Malik turned the music up. Music helped him zone out; relax more. However, the rapid thoughts began to become unhealthy. They were making a bad turn. His focus turned toward his inability to do right. How he wanted to do right, but wrong always superseded. He wanted to do right by God and Melissa, himself and his daughter, but to him it seemed like every time he felt like he was winning, there was a loss lying in the cut for him.

Malik recalled his first love. He knew he wasn't perfect, hoped she was. During a bit a few years back he'd hoped that whatever was wrong with their relationship could be repaired. Alicia had been there for him a lot in the past. She was aware of his cheating and tired of his tardiness at home. Her love for him was waning but still stronger than most marriages.

Six months before Malik's "out" date, Alicia missed every visit. Finally, she came clean and told him about the many rendezvous she had with men over the course of three years. Malik was molded, unsure of how to handle the situation. He pushed Alicia to the side, leaving his goal to do right by her incomplete.

Years before that, he denounced his position in the dope game. That was a joke, didn't last long. Again, fresh out of jail, Malik ran into an associate of his, offered him a key to the city. Needless to say, he hasn't looked back since.

There were many times Malik tried to deviate from his addictive, aggressive, and tainted behavior, yet he'd always failed. This bothered him tremendously. He thought he could achieve greatness at anything.

Malik wasn't the type of person to regret any course action he'd taken. However, no matter how flawless he tried to be, he was critical of his own flaws. This recognition of his flaws helped shape him into the person he was, of course this came with time.

One such flaw, and most detrimental, next to his greed was his thinking errors. The choices he'd made in life, were colorful, interesting, and definitely provocative. As refined as he claimed to be, his choices could've been made with a little more polish. His thoughts culminated as he approached a red light.

Reminderrr Reminderrrr—I got it if you need a friendly reminderrrr

Jay-z slapped on the inside of his truck. Malik focused hard on who would be out to sideline him so bad. He thought of all the fights, cheating women, the shootouts, near death experiences, arrests, the joint, the time he saved his friends life, when he chased a shooter away from finishing his comrade off.

"Aint that a bitch," he thought.

191

*

Melissa sat on the couch in the entertainment room of the new house. She sat silently staring at the television screen, not watching, just staring. Her thoughts consumed her. Was Malik her best choice? What better choice was there to make — no one was perfect, she had to know that. In fact she knew it first-hand. Her secret almost spiraled out of control, but was he the person she thought he was?

Thoughts dismissed, assuring herself Malik was who and what she needed and wanted. Targeted by the thirsty, being a man, standing his ground, standing for something, respect was earned in more ways than one. If there was a bulls-eye on her baby's back, she would not stand by and watch them take the shot. She knew jealousy, was a witness to the backlash of the common, irrational emotion. He was intelligent, had a kind heart, was good looking, his success was growing, almost leaving his old life behind him. The phone rang.

"Hi, baby."

"What you doin?" asked Malik.

"Thinkin bout you actually."

"Is that right."

"That's right," said Melissa. "I'm worried about you babe. I can't front. Things are getting way outta hand, don't you think?"

"I know. You at home?"

"Yeah."

"Good we need to talk, not right now doe," said Malik.

"I'll be there in a minute."

"K—I love you."

"Love you too."

Melissa flicked through the channels, cuddling herself on the chocolate sectional, doubting Malik would allow her to do any heavy lifting. She would be happy to help any way she could.

*

"I heard you was looking for me pussy?"

Damn thought Roscoe, the man brought it to his front door. In his house, nowhere to run, no games to play, this can't be life. This was what he wanted, but he froze at the element of surprise. How'd he know where he stayed?

"C'mon man I know you aint shook. I damn sho know you aint surprised."

Roscoe stared at the figure sitting on his couch. House was dark, for some reason, the voice wasn't coming from the man on the couch.

"Jermaine—you hurting my feelings fam. You making me think you was selling wolf tickets. You had to be prepared for this shit."

Roscoe reached for the Ruger in his waist. Slow— slow—slow— got it, hand reaching the grip. Tried to unlatch the safety.

Click-clack.

Malik cocked back his .40 cal.

"Sike," said Malik. "Lemme get that."

Malik walked around Roscoe, confronting him face to face. He snatched the Ruger out of Roscoe's waist, keeping his .40 trained at the throat of Roscoe. Malik flicked on a lamp.

"Sit-down."

As Roscoe sat down without a word, Tony stood up.

"Sup my dude," said Tony. "Heard you had a helluva night?"

Silence.

"Man this nigga aint no fun Malik. This can't be the one."

"Alright," said Malik. "Let's get to the bottom of this shit. Da fuck is your problem? You have been following me, blowing shit up, tried lighting my ass up. Please tell me this aint about no bitch."

Silence.

Whack.

Malik smacked Roscoe wit the ass end of the pistol.

"Naw bitch you going to tell me sumthin," Malik said angrily. "All this ho ass shit you been on—fuck it Tone let's take him to the bubble. We'll put it together foe him."

Roscoe swung a wild elbow to the face. Tony ducked the blow effortlessly. He instinctively followed up with a left hook of his own.

Whack!

Roscoe's vision impaired, white dots were everywhere.

"Bitch ass nigga! I did eight years cuz of you."

"Faggot you did eight years cuz you was thirsty ass fuck. My nigga in a chair for the rest of his life, matter of fact ... ."

Malik walked out, mumbled something into his phone, and walked back into the living room with two zip ties. Tony punched Roscoe in the back of the head, knocking him out cold. Hog-tied and bloody, Roscoe was escorted to his own damp, cold, plastic covered basement.

Malik let someone in from the back door.

"We good?"

"Oh fa sho."

"Man thanks for this my nig. Whoever said karma was a mutha fucka aint never lied."

"Aww well you know," said Malik. "Some niggas just do too much, can't escape their fate. Call me never mutha fucka, we out."

The four men laughed, as Tony and Malik cautiously exited the back door.

Water boiled in a coffee- pot, exceeding one hundred and ninety degrees. Roscoe lay flat on the plastic covered floor, shirtless, sleep. The water was handed to the orchestrator of the evening.

"AAAAAHHHHH—AAAHHHHH —AAAHHHH FUCK—FUUUUUCK," Roscoe cried.

"Oh you cryin now bitch," said a man in a wheelchair.

"AAHHHH—Fuck," Roscoe adjusted his sights facing his torturers. "James?"

"Remember me?"

Next to him stood a man dressed in black ACG boots, black Levis, black sweater, black skully, with red San Francisco Forty-Niners gloves on. Roscoe found the gloves to be most threatening for some reason. The man's face stood out above all, pasty white and greasy, like powder working at McDonald's all day. His eyes were blue as the waters in the Caribbean. He was just ill to look at. A satchel of some sort was wrapped around his waist.

"Don't ask who I am cuz you don't need to know," Pasty said. "You either hired me or, you didn't."

The man extracted a syringe filled with a throat numbing medicine that mimics Vocal Cord Dysfunction, or VCD. Slowly every scalpel, every saw, every clamp came into view on a small table behind him. James screwed on the silencer to his Walther P99.

"I'm gone help you out. I'm going to shoot you in the same places you shot me. Hopefully, you'll expire before he starts getting into the detail part of his job.

"Wait my nigg," said Roscoe. "I got cash bro. Ya'll aint gotta … ."

Whomp! Whomp!

"Can't no amount of money bring feeling to my legs cuz—let it go fam," said James. "It's over."

James wheeled out of the room, gave Pasty some dap.

"You scrate?" asked James.

"Yessir."

"Peace."

"Peace."

Roscoe cried out loud, praying to God.

                                                                            *

Forty-Eight hours earlier

Smitty stopped at H-Town bar trying to figure out his next move. He didn't know what Roscoe had against Malik. Smitty didn't even know Malik, but he figured Roscoe's hatred was beyond reconciliation. But, Smitty respected Malik. He respected him for grinding his way into legitimacy. With that thought, it was hard to shit on somebody that he knew nothing about. Somebody, he thought he would probably like if it weren't for Roscoe's manipulative ass.

What Smitty didn't know was the fact that he and Roscoe had some explaining to do. He ordered a drink.

"Lemme get a double of thirty-eight and a ice water."

"I got you," said Jimmy the bartender. "Eight dollas."

Smitty shot him a twenty.

"Bring me another one in five minutes."

As Smitty walked to the pool table, a curvaceous, gorgeous, specimen of a woman was stalking him. Smitty put three quarters in the table.

"Can I play?" asked Chanelle, sipping a V8 Splash.

Smitty was stuck. He didn't know what to say. She waited for an answer.

"Oh-yeah, fuck it. Grab a stick," said Smitty.

Chanelle strutted towards the sticks on the wall.

"Can you play?" asked Smitty.

"I used to. I haven't played in a while."

Smitty broke the rack. Not knowing what to think of the woman in front of him. Not the best looking guy on the market, noticing she looked like she'd always had the best of everything, something didn't sit right with him.

"So, what you do for a living," asked Chanelle. "Damn I didn't even introduce myself. I'm Chanelle."

She extended her manicured hand.

Smitty couldn't help but to look her over, again. Dereon hugged her waist, a red sweater wrapped itself around her favorable top-half, red sling backs revealed a couple of polished toes, slim ankles.

"Oh—yeah, I'm Smitty. Are you waiting on somebody or something?"

"No. Why you ask me that?"

"Cuz, I'm not usually this lucky," said Smitty. "Not saying you tryna knock me off. I'm just saying."

"Oh God I'm just tryna have some conversation, catch a buzz, and take my ass home. Relax homie."

Smitty was relieved, disappointed at the same time. He'd hoped she was at least for sale. Still, glad he didn't have to keep sparring with her mentally. He wasn't up to the challenge. She was too much.

"Oh-that's cool. I thought you was tryna set me up or sumthin."

He realized his mistake as soon as it poured over his lips.

"Okay. I guess that tells me what you do for a livin," she said. "Now what if I was a detective, you'd be assed out."

Smitty laughed.

"Naw you don't fit the description."

Smitty missed an easy deuce in the side pocket. The waitress was bringing him his next double. Chanelle bent over, back arched, perfect posture for the sport, giving Smitty enough to look at. Sunk her three ball in upper left corner pocket.

"I don't."

"Chanelle right?"

"Yes."

"Well F.Y.I. I don't do what you think I do, so, honestly I aint say too much of anything. Look where we at, uh nigga aint

exempt from getting set-up regardless of his occupation."
Smitty snapped back. "But you, you guessin what I do so, is that
by design or default."

"Okay then Smitty, listen at you. Sorry. You was just
actin all shy and retarded. I thought you left your player card at
the crib homie."

Smitty was feeling his 1738. Gestured toward the bar
for another, Chanelle noticed the swag change. Alert,
defensive, defenseless. Chanelle tried to bank the five ball,
missed purposely.

"Loser buy the next round?" Smitty proposed.

"Okay, well let's raise the stakes. You win—you can
come home with me. You lose, only your pocket comes with
me, and I mean the whole pocket."

Smitty didn't think twice.

"Bet."

The sexy bartender brought Smitty his double shot and
bottled water, as he was trying to win the game. Chanelle
grabbed both glasses by the rim, putting them both in front of
Smitty.

"Here go your do-it fluid," Chanelle smirked seductively.
"You might need that."

She laughed and strutted her way to the end of the
table.

Smitty was distracted. He paused and took his double
to the face. Ice water followed.

"Tre ball—cross corner," said Smitty.

He sunk that and his last four shots.

"Eight ball side pocket for game," Smitty paused for effect.

Chanelle smiled uneasily.

"Best two outta three?"

"Naw, I want my chips with dip baby. You need a drink?"

"Naw I'm good. Let's roll daddy."

The minute Smitty hit the door, he knew he'd been had. Suddenly, his vision was misty like a smoke screen. Dizzy and helpless needing help to walk, he stumbled his way to the car.

"You alright?" she asked.

"You-tell-me," he replied.

"I aint gonna lie to you. You don't look cool at all. You want me to drive?"

"Bitch, what you put in my drink?"

"What?"

Smitty dropped his keys while fumbling to get inside his Bravado.

"Dude I aint do nothing to your drink," said Chanelle. "And I don't take too kindly to what you tryna say. I thought we were gonna have a fair lil' night. But you aint bout to blame me and try to kill me bout no bullshit."

"Wait," Smitty yelled. "You right I can't drive. Just go to a room or something."

"I'm serious, drive yourself. You aint bout to put me under scrutiny. I suggest you go back in and call a cab."

Chanelle laughed to herself.

"You killed that demo."

Chanelle strutted off in her red pumps, leaving Smitty discombobulated on the sidewalk. Smitty looked for his keys.

Whack!

CHAPTER 16

Smitty woke up to a mean headache, two anonymous women were tending to his head. They watched him come to.

"I'm Jasmine," a peanut butter beauty spoke, five foot nothing, cut -off jeans shorts, white tank top.

Smitty was confused. He couldn't remember anything.

"And I'm Jackie," said another lovely girl, yellow as the sun, thick as Pinky.

"You were hit over the head by a monkey wrench. A friend saw what happened, asked for our help," said Jasmine. "Do you mind or ... ."

"Naw, I'm just tryna remem ... ."

Smitty felt a breeze at his crotch area. He was hanging limply out of his pants. He smiled.

"Damn ya'll aint gotta take it," Smitty claimed. "Ya'll can have it."

Jackie grabbed his manhood immediately.

"Can I have it?" Jackie asked. "It is a nice one."

Jackie reached under the cover behind her.

"Yes, ya'll can. And thank you. Who sent ya'll though," Smitty asked, but didn't really care.

He tried to think straight but he couldn't. Between the pain in his head and the headache, he had a hard time concentrating. He could see he was in a nice room. Refrigerator, stove, balcony, he relaxed in vain.

Jackie pulled out a butcher knife slightly longer than Smitty's manhood. She was quick, the blade was at his dorsal vein in a flash, no time to react or comprehend.

Jasmine pulled out a .22 just as fast, revealing the plot.

"Who's tryna kill Malik?" she asked.

"Who blew up his shop?" the other chimed in.

Smitty was silent. He didn't know what to say, how to react or should he react. He knew he wouldn't do anything drastic with the business end of a butcher knife on his dick. He was shook.

"Look baby, wasn't none of that shit my fault. I aint have shit to do … ."

Jasmine applied pressure.

"Aaahh shit okay."

Smitty paused. He didn't know what the right answer was, obviously they knew he had something to do with it, but how did they find him?

The bathroom door opened. The sound of a large weapon was being cocked. Juan walked out of the bathroom with a shotgun.

"Okay look," said Juan. "This is my thing. I know you had something to do with my dude shop being blown up. But we don't know you, none of us. So we figured you gotta be working for someone. But that someone is a hard fucking maggot to find. So I decided to go through you. You were my idea. I knew it couldn't have been personal to you, just a job. Plus why would you use your own car? That was dumb. It's easy to trace a license plate back to the owner. Cameras can see a long way broski. I saw the truck was in your mom's name. Wasn't hard to find you after that."

"Sounds like you know all there is to know my dude," Smitty countered.

"Uhh, not exactly," said Juan. " See, I just can't seem to find your boy. You wanna help me out?"

"No."

"Really?"

"Yeah."

"Seriously dude, deez hoes got you fucked all the way over. They know how to clean up and everything. There would be no traces of you," said Juan. "Not to mention, I'm gonna knock your muthafuckin block off if you don't speak soon! I was going to even let the ladies run it on you. So how bout it? They already paid for anyway."

Smitty weighed his options. Malik was definitely going to kill Roscoe. Roscoe would never know. Hell, he didn't even like Roscoe a whole hell of a lot in the first place. Wondered if he'd really be able to fuck after this. Smitty looked at the two ladies. He would damn sure try.

"You got thirty seconds, Smitty," said Juan. "You too tough for me boy. I don't even know what the fuck you thinking so hard for. Your life is on the line. 15,14,13 … ."

Jackie moved the tip of the blade to his scrotum sack.

"Okay bruh," Smitty said. "Damn this aint cool."

"In all fairness he light weight set you up too. That man know I aint playin."

"Alright look … ."

Smitty told it all. He didn't leave one detail out. Even told about a girl Roscoe was seeing, teaching how to shoot. Juan contemplated that for a minute, but thought nothing of it. Figured if she was around she could get it too. By the time Smitty finished Juan knew where the mama was, where the girl was, what his favorite tuck spot was, favorite hotel and more importantly what he was doing tomorrow.

"Babe, why it's so dark in here," said the woman as she walked in with a bag from Bath and Body Works.

No answer.

The woman knew her boyfriends' car was outside. Wondered if he left with somebody, but she knew he didn't have many friends. She proceeded up the stairs, still dark, cut on the lights and looked in the bedroom. No sign of her man. She turned on the television, got undressed, went to the bathroom, turned on the shower.

"Fuck."

She forgot her bag.

Walking back downstairs naked, she went to the kitchen where the bag was. Why hadn't she turned the lights on? She then grabbed the bag and heard a noise. Metal falling to the floor, someone talking to themselves, fright froze her body.

Roscoe told her his life was hectic, told her he had enemies. She didn't care she needed to rid her thoughts of an old flame. He was supposed to be temporary, but he loved hard, he was exceptionally nice to her, and she decided to stick around.

She met him a while ago at the state line liquor store, where he looked so rugged and defeated. She felt sorry for him. She offered him conversation that night. Ironically it was the day before he tried to kill Malik. He was defeated.

Later she noticed he would be driving down her street, or just in the general area. He claimed he had business over there. Never did anything creepy so she let it go.

At this moment she knew she made a mistake. Needed
to get out the house, quickly realized she didn't have on any
clothes. She walked soft and slow to the stairs. Once she
reached the bedroom, she reached behind the headboard,
grabbed a small pistol strapped to the back of it. Throwing on
sweatpants and a sweatshirt seemed like a gigantic task, heart
beating like an 808, fingers fumbling all over the cotton.
Grabbed the gun, walked out the room, down the hall, down
the stairs, into the kitchen frozen again. Pasty was at the sink
washing off his utensils wearing a pair of oversized rubber
gloves. He felt her presence.

"Hello, young lady."

He was relaxed, prepared for a righteous ending or a
sad one.

She said nothing.

"Okay, listen I'm gonna grab my things downstairs and
I'm going to leave. I'm going to leave out of the back door. You
don't have to see me anymore. You can leave when I go
downstairs."

He knew he was going to kill her, but he needed to calm
her. Fear crippled her. She stood stuck with a .380 in the palm
of her hand. He turned towards the basement. Maybe she
thought he was attacking her, maybe she snapped out of the
fear and back to the reality of the tools she heard, the tools she
saw, the man that didn't belong.

POP!

Jennifer ran downstairs, hoping her fears weren't
confirmed. Smelling blood as soon as she hit the basement
stairs, she almost gagged. Roscoe stared blankly at the ceiling,

breathing shallow, losing blood by the pint. Once he saw Jennifer he lost consciousness.

*

Malik sat in church listening to the pastor. The pastor spoke about the neglect of the elders in the black community.

"I want to apologize for my generations neglect to the black boys and young men," said Reverend Bishop. "We neglected to nurture you—to feed you the sustenance of life that you needed in order to function properly in society. Most of your fathers left you at a young age, because they didn't want to deal with your mamas—and mamas this aint a knock against you but it's hard to raise a boy to become a man, aint it? I want to apologize for the ones who were a part of your lives and raised you by giving you all that you wanted, all the PlayStation's, all the bike's, and power wheel's, not because it's wrong to shower your child with gifts, but because they didn't talk to you. They let the video games raise you, instead of teaching you what they learned from life. We neglected to tell you about the evils of material things.

"So, now as you've grown up and we're too old to receive all that you wanted, had to get it yourself," he continued. "You went about getting it the same way the next man showed you how to get it. The dope man is your son's daddy. He now has all the new toys, the fresh paint, and shiny rims, and the women and the money. And instead of a real father figure, a young man looks up to, and takes commands from the neighborhood pusher. Now as he takes his cue from this particular person he adopts nothing but sin. He adopts the wrong way to live."

Malik was floored by what was being said. He had his own viewpoint about the cycle of things as it pertains to criminal activity, but the way the preacher articulated his speech seemed like he took a glimpse into his past. Malik was ready to accept his apology. The sermon was powerful, almost brought tears to his eyes. Real is real, and that was as real as it got. Malik wasn't religious at all, but the way his life was panning out he realized the path he was on was not only self-destructive but also unnecessary. Not rich by any stretch of the imagination, Malik knew what it took to get out of the way, to become legit, hell he had his own business in his twenties. That was a blessing itself, and he did the work. The rest was just greed.

Later that night, Malik went out to eat with Melissa at Carabas. He was dipping his bread in oil, when Melissa spoke.

"So babe, what's next?"

"What you mean?"

"I mean, what are we going to do next?" she asked again. "I'm kind of scared to stick around here right now."

"What kind of nigga do you think I am?"

Malik reached inside his jacket pocket and pulled out two plane tickets, laid them on the table.

"I can't stand you," she looked at the dates. "We're leaving tonight?"

"Aint that what it say," Malik shook his head.

"Well, I aint hungry no more, lets go pack."

"Bet."

As they drove away, Malik tucked his .40 cal under the seat. He drove to the highway, headed south on I-75. His phone rang.

"Hello?"

"What it do?" asked Juan.

"Not too much just came from a dummy mission, wit my girl," said Malik. "What up?"

"Aw shit. I just needed to holler at you ma nig. Think we got a straggler."

"Wut?"

"Yeah, square business, a broad. A white broad?"

"Yeah? Where you at?"

"In my hood."

"Alright, I'm going to holler at you when I get round there."

"Peace."

"Peace."

"Baby slow down," said Melissa.

The rain was coming down pretty hard. Malik was doing eighty. Ohio's speed limit doesn't exceed sixty-five. A car swerved in front of Malik from the opposite lane. Malik hit the brake, but he slid. The car did a 360. Melissa screamed at the top of her lungs. Malik tried to straighten the wheel. He took his foot off the brake. The car came to a stop, right before a Ford pick-up truck rammed into the driver side door.

Spectators called the ambulance and some tried to help. Both Malik and Melissa were out. No one could tell if they were alive. Blood leaked from Malik's head. The steering wheel was jammed into his legs. He had his seat belt on and the air bag was deployed. Door was jammed inward. He would need the jaws- of- life to bite away the metal that threatened to become his tomb.

Melissa had no injuries apparent to the eye. However, she was knocked out as well. She slowly came to. Her neck injury crippled her ability to turn from side to side. She could barely turn to see if Malik was okay.

"Malik," she whispered.

He didn't answer.

She panicked.

"Malik," she screamed in vain.

She heard the ambulance in the distance.

"Malik—help—help is coming baby." Melissa struggled to put her hand against his face. "Please be okay Malik. I love you baby."

Just as the paramedics approached the vehicle, Malik's head fell limply in her hand.

"Oh my God."

*

"I'm sorry ma'am he's not gonna make it. He's lost too much blood. Do you know what happened?" asked Dr. Rahmour.

Jennifer broke down.

"No-o-o-o, I have no idea."

"Do you know of any family he might have?"

"No."

"Okay ma'am the police are going to want to talk to you, procedural stuff, sorry about your loss.

Detective Reese stepped up.

"I'm sorry ma'am, you're gonna have to come with us," the detective said.

They questioned her about the dead man in her house. They questioned her about Roscoe. The detectives knew he was responsible for a lot of robberies, a lot of crime period. She couldn't help them. She barely knew the man, let alone his dealings in the streets.

"He gave me a key, cuz my sister doesn't like him," Jennifer said. "She said something wasn't right about him."

"I guess your sister was right," the detective countered.

"She usually is ... ."

"Well, I guess we can chalk this anonymous man to self-defense considering what the hell he was doing in that basement. You're free to go for now, but please try to stay in the area for a while. We may want to contact you in the future."

Jennifer left the Toledo Police Safety Building. She headed home. The day's events weighed heavy on her brain, but hadn't totally set in. She needed her sister bad. Not having a chance to talk to her yet, Jennifer was lost. She pulled in, noticed the door was open, panic, anxiety, set in. She raced to the door.

"Toni?"

No one answered.

"Toni," she repeated.

"What," Toni yelled from the top of the stairs. "Why are you yelling?"

Jennifer rushed to her sister, hugging her hard.

"Oh my God you don't know what I've been through," she said.

She noticed her sister had her bags packed.

"Where are you going?"

"Gotta go to work," answered Toni. "What's wrong?"

Jennifer began to cry again.

"Oh my God Toni, that guy you didn't like, that I was seeing … he got killed last night. And, and, I-I-I killed the man that killed him … ."

Toni sat down in shock. She stared at Jennifer, couldn't believe what she was hearing. Jennifer went on to explain the rest.

"Are you okay?" asked Toni. "That's awful. I don't know what to say."

Toni sat and comforted her sister for a while. She needed to go to work to clear her mind of what she just heard.

"I take it you're not coming to work today?"

"Absolutely not."

"Okay I'll bring you some goodies when I get back."

Jennifer smiled, "Okay."

As soon as Toni arrived at work, EMU was rushing someone through the emergency room, preparing to go to surgery.

"Toni we're going to need you here in a minute," said Dr. Shareef.

Toni quickly scrubbed in. A woman rolled by on a gurney. She looked familiar, couldn't place her face. She wasn't hurt too bad probably just checking her for precaution, thought Toni. What happened next took a breath a way.

"Black male, weight 175, height 5'9, blunt injuries to the head, suffered some whip-lash, severely broken back, x-rays show spinal injuries to t-12 and l-1, some caving in the chest area, we gotta work fast people," the doctor said.

Toni turned around to administer the anesthesia.

She froze.

"Malik?"

215

Juan got the news about Malik the next day. He was already in the air, on his way to D.C. to meet Malik's former cellmate from prison. Once he landed and was on his way to the meeting he told Ibrahim about the troubles Malik was having. Ibrahim was saddened about the news. He valued Malik's friendship and truly prayed for a speedy recovery.

After all the pleasantries, it was time to get down to business. In private Malik and Ibrahim discussed price, routes, different routes, different products, expenses, who's who, timing, trust, loyalty, penalties for the lack thereof.

"Malik told me you were sharp Juan," said Ibrahim. "I like that. Here's what I'm going to do for you. I have a gift for you. How does ten holiday turkeys sound? You can get them for fifteen dollars apiece. I know you know no one is doing that, anywhere. Here's the thing, you take that deal, for the duration of our relationship the rest will come, half on consignment, half cash up front. These are all on consignment, and will be at a destination of your choice when you return. One thing though, we do this for five years, no way out after you take this pack. Not after you make enough to quit, five with the option to re-sign for a longer term, or you may bow out gracefully. But only after the five, so what's it gonna be?"

*

Tony left out of a house he'd been to many times before. He jumped in his rental car and drove off. As he turned down a backstreet, came to a stop at a stoplight, he was caught slipping.

"Rod sends his condolences," said Rod's brother.

He hid in the back seat, popped up with the gun to Tony's head.

*

Three months later, Malik was exhausted physically and mentally, but by the grace of God he was still moving around. At least that was his thoughts as he held a conversation with Juan.

"Shit everything going cool?" asked Juan.

"Shit I can't complain. Man, shit I'm still breathing. How that shit going with homeboy?" Juan gave him dap.

"That's a good look bro. I can't thank you enough. It's strange though I didn't know Muslims got down like that."

Malik laughed.

"Man niggas is silly man. They aint no different than any Christian call themselves going to church everyday swear they living right, and how their God is a forgiving God," Malik said. "What you think Allah aint a forgiving Allah?"

"Good point," said Juan. "You was always a thinking nigga."

"I'm just saying man, damn."

The two men laughed heartily. Malik gave Juan some dap before he left. Juan pulled off in an unassuming Buick Lucerne. Somehow, Malik knew that's how he'd always remember his man.

Then Tony pulled up in his truck. Malik walked off the porch he was sitting on and jumped in the car with Tony.

"Aye Malik man, I just want you to know man, I appreciate you dog. You're a real friend. I been around a lot of niggas man, and I can only say a few been my real nigga and you one of em."

"Da fuck you so emotional for?" asked Malik.

"Now did I ask you that when you sat me down on your birthday nigga," Tony replied. "Naw man I just wanted to let you know that man and tell Rene' I love her cuz."

Malik began to worry. He really wanted to know what was going on now. Tony turned in the car to give Malik a hug. Half of Tony's head was blown off.

After three months, Malik finally opened his eyes from being in a coma.